CAPTURED BY THE MOB

BIANCHI CRIME FAMILY

C.M. STEELE

THE STEELE PRESS

CAPTURED BY THE MOB

Nero: As the Underboss and enforcer for the Bianchi Family, I've got my hands full. When dealing with my enemies, I'm quick, efficient, and I never slip up. That's until one beauty accidentally gets in the way, seeing more than she should. I can't let her go, and I can't end her, so I do the only thing I can...

I take her captive.

Mariana: I thought my day couldn't get any worse. I sucked at my job and was about to be homeless until I had to go knocking on the wrong door. When he opened the door and dragged me in, I thought I was a goner, but it's not that simple. He has other plans for me.

For now, he's my captor.

1

Nero

"ANY PROBLEMS that I need to be made aware of?" Dom asks as we sit in his office, sipping our coffee. We're having our weekly morning meeting before we handle our day-to-day operations. I live less than a mile down the road from his estate, which makes it easy for these early-ass days.

"Nothing on my end, but you know, the day's only just begun."

Just as the words are out of my mouth, the office door bursts open. Our eyes go straight to the door and to the man standing there. "We have a problem. A major discrepancy, as a matter of fact," Niccolò blurts out in a rush of words as he storms into Domani's office with his dress shirt rumpled like he's been up all freaking night. I set my coffee down and stare at him. If I didn't know better, I'd say he'd found someone to warm his bed, but the man lives like a hermit surrounded by his books.

"Well, good morning, brother." Dom raises his hand,

stopping his brother from going off the handle. It's only seven, and Niccolò looks as if he's gonna jump out of his skin with anxiety if he doesn't get this off his chest.

"Sorry—good morning, Dom, Nero." I acknowledge his greeting with a nod and then go back to my cup of coffee. I have a feeling I'm going to need it. Nico's not prone to outbursts or looking so damn disheveled, so all hands need to be on deck for this one.

"I'd offer you some coffee, but I'm guessing you've already had an entire pot." I have to bite the inside of my cheek to hold back the chuckle. "So now that we got that out of the way—the who, what, and whys."

He adjusts his glasses, pushing them back up his nose and then takes a deep breath before beginning his tale. "Well, I noticed that the money from the Eastside Market has been short. Looking back at the records from the shop owner, money has been missing every month. Our runners don't know that we get a report from the client as well. Comparing the two, it's clear as day that Eddie Walsh has been skimming off the top and handing in false reports."

"Okay. Are you sure?" Nico gives his brother the *are you kidding me* look. The man knows his numbers to the point of some *Rain Man*-type shit. If he says it's wrong, then it is.

"Fine. Where is this asshole?"

Nico sets a document down on Dom's desk. "I don't know exactly where he's hiding out at. That's not my area." He looks at me and then back to Dom. "I have his contact info, but I don't know where he stays. I noticed he started looking like a dopehead the last time he made a deposit."

So there's a chance he could be hiding anywhere. I'll sniff that fucker out. It's my job, after all. I'm the underboss and one hell of an enforcer. I've found and dealt with more of our enemies than anyone else.

"Give Nero his number, and then you go back and get some fucking sleep. You look like shit." Damn, those are fighting words in this family. We all take pride in dressing well. The clothes make the man. No one would take us seriously if we strolled in looking like Nico right now.

"I thought getting married and having your heir would make you a happier man," Nico mutters, adjusting his clothes a bit and brushing his hands down his suit jacket. Again, I have to hold back the laugh that's tickling the back of my throat.

"I'm fucking ecstatic when there aren't problems taking me away from my queen." Dom turns to address me. "You know what to do, Nero." He hands me the number on a piece of paper.

"Yes." I nod and make a note to run a tracker on his number. There's too much going on to handle the matter at the moment. I keep my seat while Nico leaves, closing the door behind him.

"Damn, Nico needs to loosen up." I adjust my sleeves and shake my head. If anyone else had said that to Dom, he would have them pinned to the wall with a gun in their mouth, but since they're both my cousins, I get away with saying it.

"Tell me about it. That stress is going to send him to the hospital. I don't need this added problem. I need to head over to my Northside distillery and check on the plans for the expansion."

"Sounds good. I'll make sure to have this taken care of by the end of the day." I'm not one to fail on assignments, even if it means taking me away from my usual days at our investment firm.

"I know you will."

We shake hands and leave his office just in time for his

wife to come up to us in the entryway. "On your way out?" she asks me as Dom drags her to his side. The man is obsessed with his wife, and it's plain for everyone to see. Not that I'm complaining, because I like Aria.

"I have some business to handle. See ya later, Aria," I say.

"Be careful, Nero," she warns me. She's a sweetheart, and my cousin is lucky to have her.

"I will do my best." I wink and walk out of the house, hopping in my SUV to get my duties handled. I have to go into the office and make my presence known before I can split and drop the son of a bitch robbing us blind. After looking at the discrepancies, I'm shocked that he got away with it for so long. A junkie isn't the kind of person to be meticulous. Call it a gut instinct, but I doubt he's working alone.

Pulling into my parking spot, I head into the office. We keep a minimum amount of security in the building to prevent our own issues should our alibis be needed.

My assistant is on me with his clipboard, itching to give me the list of shit I have to tackle before I can get to my boss's request. "Mr. Bianchi, you have three new messages this morning from Mr. Rodgers. He wants to know if you have time for a meeting."

"Lord, does that man try my patience." I rub my temples. "Carson, set it up for noon. He'll get an hour of my time to give me what he has, and not a minute more." That man drives me bananas. He's so damned anal about everything, especially when it comes to finances. Hell, he makes Niccolò look chill, except my cousin is a lot better at his job. Niccolò's his boss, but since I'm the one who determines which projects we fund, he needs to go through me.

"Yes, sir," Carson says, tapping his tablet with his stylus and super proud that he's able to check something off his list. He's another one who is a perfectionist.

"I need a cup of coffee." His face screws up in surprise, so I answer his unasked question. "My cup went cold this morning." He knows that when I meet with my cousin, I usually forgo my morning dose of caffeine.

"Yes, sir."

I slide into my office, closing the door behind me and hoping that no one else breaks my concentration. The first thing to do is to track Walsh down, take him out, and dispose of his remains before anyone notices. Still, that must wait until I handle the list of projects and reports waiting for me.

I spend my morning going over all my duties for the office, having Carson fill my coffee twice. It's just one of those days. A headache builds between my eyes so I set the last cup to the side, focusing on my work.

A knock at my door twenty minutes before my meeting with Rodgers irritates me. If it's that pipsqueak, I might wring his scrawny neck.

"Come in." My assistant walks in looking a little rattled.

"Everything okay?"

"Sir, I have a family emergency."

"Yes?"

"Yes, my mom's cat tripped her and she's on the way to the hospital." Damn, that's rough. His mother loves her cat. I happen to be a dog person, but I know they just love to get under your feet as you're walking, and Carson's mother isn't young anymore so the risks of serious injury are much greater.

"I'm sorry. I hope she's going to be okay," I offer my

sympathies because he looks so nervous to ask to leave early. He's worked for me for two years, and I don't believe he's ever left early or taken a day off.

"Thank you. I hope so too."

"Go on and get out of here. I can deal with Rodgers. Let me know if you'll be in tomorrow when you figure it out."

"Thank you again, Mr. Bianchi." I nod, and he rushes out. That's good, because having one last person running in and out of the office is better for my method of disappearing for a few hours. I have ways to go unnoticed; however, it does make it easier.

My private line rings, and this is for the other business I need to handle today. "Bianchi," I answer.

"Boss man, it's Bingo."

I know who it is even though I don't store names in this phone. It's a burner phone that we have hundreds of, having fallen off a shipment headed for Chicago eight months ago. Of course, the manifests with the serial numbers on them disappeared as well. How fucking convenient.

"Hey, Bingo, where is Eddie Walsh?" He's one of our guys who is in the know about almost everything. We call him that because instead of saying yes, his answer is always "bingo." The man is a bit weird but is a dedicated son of a bitch.

"Walsh? Last I saw him was around two in the morning. He was on his way back from the strip club in Hinsdale. He said he had to wait at a home in the southwest suburbs to pay off a debt. He said if he did the job, he and the guy would be square."

"What kind of job?"

"I don't know. He just told me it would be fun, and in that creepy fucking predator tone he has sometimes. I'm guessing it's one of Gordon's potential prostitutes with some nose candy for him to push." More like sniffing up his own fucked-up nose.

"Do you have the place?"

"Bingo." He reads off the address, and then my alarm on my computer goes off. I have a meeting with Rodgers to get to.

"Stay strong and do your job," I tell him and end the call. So Walsh is holed up in a home in the southwest suburbs. I tap my pen on my desk and then head down to the conference room for my meeting with Rodgers.

An hour later and not a minute more, I'm up and out of the conference room, bored to tears. The man needs to get a sense of humor—even just a bit. I head back into my office and pack up my shit.

I pretend to be working when I get a call at the office from Carson. He's going to be out the next two days because his mother's hand and ankle are sprained, and she'll need some help around until his sister can return to town. It's fine because the place runs like a well-oiled machine that brings in a hundred million dollars annually in revenue.

Slipping out the back exit from my office and down the private staircase that leads to another vehicle of mine. From this angle, my car can't be picked up by any of the surveillance cameras. I don't use a digital map and this ride isn't built with a GPS, so after using a paper map, I head south.

The drive is a long one, so it takes me two hours to get there in this fucking shitty traffic. I picked the wrong time to leave, but I didn't want the fuck to leave if he happened to get wind that we're onto his scam. It's nearly bumper to bumper until you get past the city itself, then the roads open up. Why does Chicago traffic suck so fucking much?

Once I arrive in the poor, run-down suburban area, I

scope it out for any signs of security. There looks to be little to no security anywhere which isn't surprising.

This area had once been affluent, but all it took was a lot of drugs to turn that around. It's one of the shittier parts of town, so I search the area for anyone suspicious, going about it methodically before I approach the house where my target is waiting. I spend a good while watching as no one comes and goes from that house. Thankfully, most of the homes are vacant or boarded up nearby, leaving fewer potential witnesses. Not that anyone would say a word because snitching is frowned upon in this drug ridden area.

It's four in the afternoon when I finally decide it's time to make my move. I'm creeping down the block to the house he's holed up in when my attention is divided by a woman. I spot an angel coming my way. The sun creates a halo around her long, wavy reddish-brown hair pulled back in a messy ponytail that's coming undone. It's the middle of May, but the sun's beating down with a heatwave which creates a dewy glow on her face, brightening up her rosy cheeks. Heaven help me, she looks thoroughly fucked, and if I get my way she will be.

Fuck me. My dick stiffens in my suit pants to the point of pain, so I do my best to look away. I should just duck my head and make sure she doesn't see me, but I need to steal another glance. Thankfully, she's oblivious to my stare as she moves to a parked vehicle just across the street, kitty-corner from my location. She's in a pair of plain khaki pants and a dark green polo with a logo on the breast pocket. Despite having a large chest, the logo is hard to make out with the sun beaming down.

She sits down in the car, taking a long drink of water before making some notes on her pad of paper. Using my burner phone, I zoom in with the camera and then write down her plate number that I plan to pull the records on very shortly.

"Priorities, remember your priorities," I say, trying to follow through on my objective. I'll deal with this piece of shit, and then I'll find her again. Business first, and then I'm going to find a way to introduce myself to my future bride. One look, one unaware swipe of her hair behind her ear, and my soul belongs to that woman; it doesn't take more to know she's mine.

Ignoring my lust, I head off to where I need to be, slip on my leather gloves, and screw on the suppressor. I enter through the sliding glass patio door in the back yard, which is surprisingly unlocked. Fucking crackheads are too stoned to remember things like that. I can smell the piss-soaked floors from the kitchen, and I do my best to hold my breath.

Creeping through the house, I find my target peeking through the front window, waiting, unaware that I'm feet from him with my gun in hand. When his eyes turn on me, my gun is pressed into his chest.

"It looks like we have a problem, Walsh. You've been stealing from us." His eyes turn into saucers as he processes what's happening.

The doorbell rings, and I freeze. "You be quiet," I snarl with my finger to my lips for him to shut it. I still have to question this asshole. He's not working alone. Perhaps that's who he's meeting with to fuck us over some more. Well, I got a bullet for that person too if they're in the slightest bit involved with this piece of dog shit.

He starts shouting, and I see eyes peeking through the window. Fucking hell. I pop him with the back of my gun against Walsh's head, dropping him to his knees, and open the door to welcome my very unwelcome guest, who better have answers for me. When her frightened eyes meet mine, I know I fucked up.

2

Mariana

Earlier that day…

"Just one more try—please, Mr. Gordon," I beg my boss. I've been a total disappointment to myself and this company. I just wanted to make more money and get the hell out of the office because I don't trust the way he looks at me.

"Girl, I'm not running a charity." More like a scam. I bite my tongue because I need money, and I need it like yesterday. I should have kept my old job, even though my last boss was a creep. Now I've been black-balled and forced to take a cold-call, door-to-door sales job for a guy who makes my old boss look like a complete gentleman.

"Please. I need this job." Frankly I'm terrible at it, but my rent is due, and this job pays quickly if people sign up for our solar power panels. "I'll do better."

"Better? Anything is better than nothing," he mocks.

True, I haven't had a single sale in the three days that I've been walking from house to house, but it's not that easy to ask someone to get something they don't need and to get all of their personal information.

"The people are so mean. I didn't see the no-soliciting sign, and he yelled at me for being an idiot." It was terrible. I cried for about twenty minutes and then had to pull myself together, but I had no will to make it through the other houses.

"What happened to the other houses? You're supposed to schmooze them. You're a fucking knockout. They should be falling at your feet." His eyes land on my breasts, ogling my tits that are on the larger side for my frame. I slowly take a step back and toss my ponytail in front of my chest, covering my breasts.

"They all have no-soliciting signs on their doors. Even the other guys only got one home each," I point out because they've been at this a lot longer than I have, and they're struggling as well. The market is currently over saturated and underwhelming as a whole.

"One is better than what you're pulling in. Well...." He pauses, tapping his finger on his chin before raking his eyes up and down my body. "You need a less-expensive neighborhood. I'll give you one more chance, but you better come back with a sale or two or you're gonna find another way to work for your money."

"What?"

He snatches a piece of my hair between his fingers and rubs it before continuing with a smug grin. "You heard me, girl. Don't play innocent. Get your ass out there, or get lost and don't come back."

I pull back and mutter a thank you. If I don't come back

with a sale, I'll run away and maybe head to a shelter or something. From the look in his eyes and the bold threat, there's no denying that he's serious. I use my phone and look up any places for women. It's a long shot, but there are several. I call the first one and find that they're at capacity. Living in a major city, I should have known better than to fall behind on my bills. However, running out of money, I don't have much choice. I get in my less-than-adequate vehicle and check the area he wants me to canvass. Fuck— there goes the last of my gas money.

I stop at the local Walmart and scoop up some non-perishable snacks so I can survive living out of my car until I land a job to feed myself. I see a sign down the road hiring now for waitresses. I'll stop by in the morning after I attempt to land just one sale. I need money today. Even if I got hired today, it would take at least a few days to start working.

Once I load my shopping cart with twenty dollars' worth of unhealthy snacks and a case of water, I head to the checkout counter. It takes every ounce of willpower to stay to my budget, but I make it work. *I really need a sale today.*

Why is everything falling apart for me? First, my parents sell their house the day I turn eighteen and head out on a road trip in an RV, only to die falling off a cliff. If I didn't know better, I would have sworn they planned it, but since they lived their lives on the whim there's no doubt that it was truly an accident.

I'm alone, broke, and living in a run-down apartment on the city's Southside that cost more than it's worth.

All the way to the south suburb neighborhood, I'm practicing my spiel. "'Hello, I'm with Sunshine Energy. May I have just a moment of your time?' No. No. No. 'Hello, I'm Mariana and I'm with Sunshine Energy. Do you have high energy bills? Would you like to save thousands a year while saving the environment?'"

This is a mess. Okay. So I'm going to be living in my car.

A couple hours later, I know that I'm screwed. Two houses that aren't boarded up remain on the block, and it's time to call it a night. This area is known for unsavory characters that come out after dark, so it's now or never. I saw a vehicle pull into the garage not thirty minutes ago, so I know someone is going to be home and that's my target. I might breakdown and beg for them to sign up. No, that's not true because I don't have a saleswoman bone in my body. I read books where women are tough, but I don't have that mettle.

Taking a deep breath, I walk up the cracked walkway which could use massive repairs. I ring the bell whose housing is broken and open wires are visible, waiting for someone to answer. Then, there's a scuffle and I hear glass crashing, and I jump back, stumbling and hitting the porch beam. It rattles, stunning me for a moment.

What if someone got hurt trying to answer the door? I peek through the window and call out. That's when a shout of help comes from inside, and I see a man with a gun pointed at the man on the ground. Shit. "Run," I whisper to myself, but I'm frozen to the spot. The door opens and before I get a chance to run, a pair of hands drag me into the house.

I'm gonna die.

The man on his knees, bleeding from his head while the man with the gun glares at me. He grabs the guy by his ratty-looking shirt and snarls, "See what you did? This girl has to pay for your actions. If you'd have shut your mouth, she could have been safe to carry on." He presses the gun to the man's head and I turn my face as the gun goes off. It's muffled, but there's no doubt the man on the ground is dead and I'm next.

He's gonna kill me.

The sexy bastard with a gun is gonna shoot me. Sexy? Have I lost my mind? I believe I have. Suddenly, the room spins as all the blood has left my brain and the room darkens. Strong arms wrap around me before I hit the ground. I barely make out that it's the guy with the gun and gun-metal gray eyes as I pass out.

I wake up, sitting in someone's lap. "You're finally awake."

I sigh and snuggle a little closer until reality hits me like a ton of bricks. "What happened? Did I just dream everything? Who are you? Where am I?"

I look up into those sexy gray eyes and gasp. I'm in the arms of the guy with the gun. "Oh my Go—" I move to jump off him, but he tightens his hold. "You're going to kill me, aren't you?"

"Your actions will determine mine," he whispers as if I'm a skittish animal, brushing the hair off my face and tucking it behind my ear ever so tenderly. A shiver filled with a mixture of unexplainable and uncomfortable emotions rushes through my body.

"What do I have to do?" What does he want with me?

"What were you doing here?" he snarls, cupping my chin and holding my face firmly in his grip. He's mad, but then again, I interrupted him. "Were you here to meet that piece of shit? Off up that delicious body?"

"I'm a solar energy sales rep. I came to sell solar panels to the neighbors," I confess, shaking as my response flows from my lips. His eyes are so pretty that I have a hard time concentrating on the fact that I'm in a monster's embrace. Did he just compliment me?

"And you just happened to knock on this door?" he growls, sliding his hand lower to my throat. He doesn't squeeze; it's as if he's caressing me but I can feel his fingers on my pulse. Our eyes stay on each other, and my heart does a flip for some strange reason. Why? Maybe it's the adrenaline flowing through me.

I break the connection and answer, "It was my second to last house."

"Okay." I can't tell if he believes me or not, but I hope he does. "So what's going to happen, Ms. Conlon—or do you prefer Mariana?" Fuck if I know. Is he giving me an option? Shit, he has my ID. I'm so in trouble.

"I'll be quiet. I promise I won't say a thing. I don't want to die," I plead. His expression goes from soft to hard, grimacing as if he doesn't trust me to keep quiet. I'll never speak of it again if he lets me walk out of here.

He cups my chin and gives me a deep, penetrating stare. "I'm going to give you a chance to go home. Don't talk to anyone, or you'll pay for it."

"I promise. I'll be good and never mention it to anyone. I'm so sorry." I move my body again, but he holds me still and reaches down by his feet. Fear dances up my spine, and I become rigid beneath his grip.

Sitting firmly and straight in his arms, I feel the hard ridge of something pressed against my ass. I can't be sitting on his gun. Am I? I move my hand under and am completely shocked. That's not his gun, although I'm sure he gets rounds off all the time. Holy fuck. He's carrying a massive weapon.

"Sorry," I whisper as a groan comes from him. I was still feeling it up. What's wrong with me?

"Don't set off my other gun. It doesn't help that you have your sexy ass on me. I'm not going to violate you. Just relax, Mariana. Here—drink this." Goodness, why does the way he says my name turn me on? This is the worst place to be and the wrong person to get aroused by.

It's clearly Gatorade, but he opened it; so what if it's poisoned? "What is it?"

"What does it look like?" he bites out, getting annoyed by my question.

"Gatorade."

"Well, then? Drink it," he barks out.

"Okay," I answer, bringing it to my lips, but not taking a sip yet because I can't take my eyes off him.

"Drink. You need to feel better." I cock my brow up at this guy who's threatened to kill me, and here he is worrying about my health. It's bizarre, and so is the feeling coursing through me as his thumb rubs my arm in a slow, soothing motion. A shiver races up my spine.

I take a drink, a small one, because I don't actually like it. "More."

"I don't like Gatorade," I reply like I'm at a five-star resort and not at the mercy of a killer. He's probably going to get very pissed. I meet his eyes and I don't see annoyance or anger; he doesn't look upset at all.

"Maybe a different brand? Powerade?" Is he serious?

"No. I don't like salty drinks. I'm fine. I really just want to go home and sleep. I swear I don't know who you are, or that man, either." My eyes scan the room, but I don't see him anywhere. He was dead on the floor before I collapsed.

"Fine, but I will know if you tell anyone."

"I swear, I won't say a word," I plead, crossing my fingers over my heart in the shape of a cross.

He grasps my chin harder than earlier, turning it so our

noses nearly brush against each other. "Not a word, you hear me? Or else."

A part of me wants to reach up and kiss those tense, frowning lips, and the other half is telling me to run like the wind. "Of course, sir."

He clears his throat, which draws my attention to his thick neck and broad shoulders. He's got me by at least hundred and fifty pounds and yet, he's holding me so tenderly. This man is too damned good looking for my own good and messing with my damn flight or fight instincts. "Where is your vehicle?"

"Around the corner," I mutter.

"Is there someone waiting for you at home?" I should say yes, because that means he might worry that someone would come looking for me and let me go.

Slowly, I slide off his lap and take a deep breath before telling the truth. "No one."

"Drive carefully." I arch my brow, wondering why he's being kind to me when I'm clearly a liability. Is he lulling me into a false sense of security? I walk to the door with him. He holds it open and adds, "Oh, and sweetheart, keep your mouth shut."

"Yes, sir." I hurry out of the house and down the street without looking back. My feet don't seem to want to move, but I do anyhow. Why does this feel wrong, leaving him? I don't know his name and he just killed a man in front of me, so the only thing to do is to be grateful and flee as fast as possible.

I start my car and drive carefully so I don't get pulled over. He might be watching me, and if the cops stop me, he could believe I told them. Shit, I wonder if someone's following me. I dart my eyes to the rearview mirror and check for him or one of his buddies. I'm sure a man like him has men at his disposal, but I didn't see a single person with him.

On the drive all the way back to my apartment, I'm a shaking mess and forget all about not making another sale. What am I supposed to do now? I have to pack as much as I can into my car without stuffing it because I'll need somewhere to sleep. What can I take in the drop of a hat?

I condensed my life the day my parents booted me from the house the day I turned eighteen, so I don't have a lot to take, but my old faithful isn't a large sedan. It's a compact car. I don't have time to make something to eat, not that I feel like eating anyway. Still, it would have been nice to have one last hot meal.

I stuff my trunk and half of the back seat before driving away from my apartment. I see a car behind me, following at a short distance, but then it turns off onto a side road. Goodness, I'm paranoid. The women's shelter isn't too far from here. All I have to do is make it inside and stay there while I search for a job.

I park my car in their roughly twenty-car lot, snagging my purse and tossing it over my shoulder before locking the doors.

A sigh falls from my lips as I grab the handle, knowing I'm about to ask for someone's generosity while doing my best not to cry. At the counter is a pretty lady who smiles up at me without any judgement in her eyes. "How can I help you?"

"Hello, I was wondering if you still have an available bed for me?"

"Is it just you, miss?" she asks, looking behind me which makes me do the same. I'm grateful that there's no one else behind me. The fear of being followed hasn't left my head, although I'm not sure I'd be totally upset if it was that big brute who cradled me like I was precious. Something about his touch lives in my bones.

"Yes." My voice shakes, betraying my fear.

"Is everything okay? You seem shaken up."

"It's just been a crazy day," I confess, and she nods, understanding that I can't say more than that.

"Well, let me give you a tour of the place. I'm Amy, by the way. It's free here, but we do ask that you help with keeping your area clean or volunteering your time to the kitchen or with the children." The price is right, and I'm grateful for the warm bed to sleep in.

"That sounds great." We walk around for an hour and end at where I'll be sleeping. Honestly, I'm so appreciative that I don't have to sleep in my car and I'm happy to have just a simple cot. "I need to head to my car to grab a small bag of clothes, but I'll be right back."

"Okay. Things will get better," Amy says, rubbing my arm.

"Thank you. I just need to find a job. I'm tempted to look outside the state."

"We have people that come in once a week for job consultations."

"That's amazing."

"Now, go get your things, sweetie." She pats my arm and then nods. I smile and give her a silent thank you before rushing outside to grab my things. I can't help but look in both directions to see if I've been followed. Damn it, I can't see anyone, but the sun's glare is in my face as it starts to set. Shit. I hurry and dash back inside, getting a curious look from Amy.

I smile and walk over to my bed and small table. Getting comfortable, I pull out my phone and start searching for work. A call comes in from my former boss, and I let it go to voicemail. There's no way I'm answering. As far as I'm concerned, I no longer work for him and he can harass someone else. Two minutes later, a voice message pops up on my phone.

I press play as I bring the phone to my ear. *I knew you couldn't do it. Your ass owes me. Get back here before I make you pay even more than just on your knees. You will be found, so you might as well make it easy on yourself.* I press the stop button. There's nothing else I want to hear.

Although it's filthy, I don't delete it in case I need it for legal reasons, but I try to put it from my mind and tuck my phone in my pocket as I hunt down the staff to see if they could use a hand.

Three hours later, my belly is semi-full, my hands are wrinkly from washing all the pots and pans, so now it's time for bed. I lie down and close my eyes. *His* eyes immediately pop into my head. Goodness, why am I remembering the way the flecks of gold in his eyes shone like a diamond with so many facets? His gruff exterior should be sending fear through me, but my body doesn't care.

Heat flows through me, wondering what it would be like to have him take that strong, firm mouth of his and plant kisses all over my skin. It's insane, so I shake my head and open my phone to scroll Facebook. I don't know why; I have a dozen or so friends, and there isn't much from the past two days except an insane amount of ads for shit I can't afford.

A friend request pops up, but I ignore it because there's no image. They shoot me a DM, and I check it. *I will get to you one way or another. -P.G.*

Goodness, it's my old boss.

Fucking asshole doesn't understand that I'll never submit to selling my pussy for money. A sick feeling strikes me when it comes to mind. He's probably done this before. A shiver of revulsion rushes through my body.

The lights in the facility go off, which means it's time for me to turn off my phone. I do so, setting it on the charging station in the corner of the room with a few other phones, and then I head back to my cot and cover up as fatigue fills my bones and my eyes grow heavy.

3

Nero

THE SECOND I let her go, I want to drag her back and not because she saw what she shouldn't have. It was so fucking stupid to let her go, but I had work to do, so I sent Enrico to keep tabs on her while I dealt with my mess.

I'd been so entranced with the color of her eyes that I forgot she'd just seen me kill the rat bastard at my feet. Instead, I scooped her up in my arms and held her tightly to me as I shot Enrico a message to pick up some Gatorade on his way to help. He brought the drink and then moved the asshole to the trunk of my car before cleaning up the mess. After using solvent and disappearing from sight, my sweet woman finally rouses.

My little nosy girl had stumbled on to my business and into my soul. She woke up in my arms, bright gray eyes staring up at me, confused, until the fear filled her. We have nearly the same color although mine are darker.

I snatched her work stuff that she had with her because I couldn't just let her off that easily, even stealing her ID because I can't have her running off. From the expression on her face, I could see that I wasn't the only one affected. Her body felt me, knowing that I'm dark and dangerous, but tempting.

I have to call Dom. He's gonna be pissed about all of this. I royally fucked up. Still, I'm going to make it right, even if I have to revert to some less-than-polite actions when it comes to Miss Conlon. Tying her to my bed and licking her from head to toe comes straight to my mind and my cock agrees.

I dial his number as I hit the road and onto the expressway far away from the loser's hideout. Everything has been scrubbed and with no cameras on the place, we're good. I dump the body in our personal cremation chamber which is much closer to home. The only thing that's a problem is my sudden obsession.

On the fifth ring, Domani answers, "What's up, Nero?"

I sigh and let it out. "I fucked up. While I was dealing with the prick, I was witnessed."

"What the fuck do you mean you have a witness? Get rid of them," Dom roars out.

A rush of anger bores deep down into my soul, and I want to snap at my cousin and boss. "I thought we didn't hurt innocents?"

"Since when is there an innocent in that area?" That's fucking true. It's a slum, and most people in the area are dealers, users, and much more.

"She's a sales rep from a solar company." I hear a pause on the other end, because he knows damn well it would take a lot to hurt a woman. She'd have to do something to his queen or son to earn that sentence.

"Solar company?" Dom questions. I thought the same

thing. What is she doing in an area that would have that shit stolen the second it was installed?

"Yeah, authentic and everything. She's going door-to-door and shit, like it's fucking safe." I can't stand the idea that she does that for a living. There are too many fucked-up people that she could run into, myself included.

"Damn it. What's really going on, Nero? I get you don't want to hurt her, but we can't do nothing." That, I understand more than anything.

"We can't hurt her," I snap. He laughs at me. Does he suspect that I'm a goner? "Wait, Dom. I have a plan, but you're not going to like it."

"What is it?" I can almost see him rolling his eyes through the phone.

"I'm going to keep her hostage and change her mind," I explain. It's much more than that. I'm going to have her screaming my name as she comes for me.

"What?"

"Let's just say I can't hurt her," I confess. My stomach burns with the idea of harming even a single hair on her head.

"This is on you, Nero," Dom points out. Something I can't forget.

I hear someone in the background when Dom adds, "I've got to go; the queen is summoning me."

"Okay. I'll talk to you later," I chuckle out because she has him by the balls, but I'm not too different I begrudgingly admit to myself.

I drive to work and sneak up to my office, grabbing my things and stopping down in Rodgers' office knowing he's still working. I hand him the signed documents that I finished before I even left. He grins from ear to ear which is a first.

"Get out more, Rodgers. I'm going home for the night."

I turn to leave when he calls out. "Thank you, Mr. Bianchi." I nod and continue out of the building to my usual SUV. Like Dom, I have drivers on occasion, but I prefer to drive myself around.

My first stop is to see Mariana and take her. I'm driving toward her apartment when Enrico calls me. "What's up?"

"She booked it out of here, filling her car with shit like she's leaving town." Damn it.

"Did you follow her?"

"Yeah, but then I lost her. There's another problem. I went back to her apartment to see if I could find anything, but there were several men looking for her in her apartment. I overheard them, and they were trying to kidnap her." Damn—my woman is having a very bad day. Once I locate her, I'll be fixing her problems.

"Find out who they are. I'll be dealing with them in due time." Each one will die at my hand.

"Understood. What about her?"

"I'll deal with her. I've stolen access to her location on her cell phone. I'll be able to find her in the next twenty minutes." I did it while she was still passed out, making my life a lot easier.

"I don't think she's going to be an issue. I'm guessing she wasn't running from you, but from the guys who showed up." I'm betting on it, too.

"It doesn't matter. I'll be speaking with Miss Conlon soon. I can't just let her go freely."

"Yes, Nero."

"Find out who those assholes are."

"On it." I click the end button and toss my phone on the seat of my vehicle. I have a plan, and I will make it work. I have a body to dispose of, and now isn't the time to forget what brought me out here in the first place. Killing Walsh immediately hadn't been my initial plan because I needed to know who he was working with, but after the fucking trouble he caused with Mariana, he just had to go. I'll figure out who he was dealing with once I get home.

After getting rid of the little shit, I return my focus to the only witness. I run the software and locate her with ease. She's on the far Southside of the city. As I drive, the location begins to get more accurate. I'm just two blocks away from her. This isn't a great neighborhood either, but it's better than the shithole we met in. I get closer and finally spot her vehicle in a small lot.

Exiting my vehicle, I take a peek inside. She's not in it, but all of her things are. The lot's attached to a woman's shelter. As I approach the front door which has no windows, there's a sign that clearly states **Men will be let in after verification.**

Not wanting anyone to know I've been around here, especially her because she might try to run again, I cool my heels and think. Sitting in my car, I debate my next moves.

Fuck, I hate that she has to sleep in some damn shelter. Still, knowing she's safe inside, I can deal with other matters. I don't want to give away my position just yet because I need to have everything organized, so I drive away, but not before slipping a tracer tag on her vehicle, just in case she has her phone off.

Deciding to check out her apartment and look for any clues to who these fuckers are, I drive into the city. I park around the back of the building and quietly enter through the fire escape. Once inside her place, I see what Tony meant; it's fucking ransacked. My blood boils knowing that she has someone after her.

I go through her belongings and check out all the little

trinkets she didn't pack. I'm betting from her present situation that she couldn't take these things with her, so I'll have my guys clear out her belongings tomorrow in dressed full moving gear with equipment just in case those fuckers come around again. In her bedroom, the remaining clothes are scattered about, including those in her hamper. The man in me knows it's terrible, but I steal a pair of her panties, bringing them to my nose. Yep, fuck me. My dick jerks and comes to life under my slacks. I tuck them in my pocket for later and go about the place.

Once I'm satisfied that I'm not going to learn anything else, I drive back home and make preparations for tomorrow. There's a lot to do before I nab my queen, including make sure she has everything females need.

A knock at my door stops the plans, and I find it's my cousin, Domani with his brow raise and frown on his mug. "You didn't come to dinner, so I'm assuming you're still dealing with our little problem?" he says, looking around my entryway for my little woman.

"Not quite."

"She's not here?" he tosses out with an air of concern.

"No. Come on in." I walk into the foyer, and he follows, closing the door behind him. "She's in a women's shelter on the Southside."

"What the fuck is she doing there?" I get that tone because he'd never leave Aria in that kind of situation, but our girls aren't the same. Her family provided for her, but my girl doesn't have any family it seems or if she does, they're dead to me. I'll never respect anyone who treats my woman so poorly.

"Hiding out," I answer, running my hands over my face because I know where his mind is leading him.

"Do you think she ratted us out?" I can see his temper

building because there's a lot on the line if she does, which I know she won't. Call it gut instinct, but my woman wouldn't do that to me. I felt the attraction vibrating between us. I might not know women, but I can read the body language of my targets as they face their potential demise.

"No. She had someone creeping by her place looking for her. Enrico's getting me what I need on that, but she packed and left her place in minutes after getting home."

"So whoever they are, they were coming for her. Do you think they were tailing her before this evening's fuckup?" He's still pissed about my error and reminding me of it.

"No, but they were expecting her at the end of her workday, so I'm guessing that's why they didn't get there until well after she fled the apartment. They trashed the fucking place so whatever the reason she ran, I doubt it has to do with us."

Dom shakes his head, frustration written with the grimace plastered on his face. "Something isn't adding up. She's in a shitty neighborhood, trying to sell solar panels, and then some fucks are at her door looking for her."

"What are you thinking it's about?"

"I don't know, but I don't like it. I want you to handle this asap, and no more fuckups."

My phone interrupts his angry command. I check it and see it's fucking important. "It's Enrico."

"What's up? I'm gonna put you on speaker because I have Dom here with me too."

"Okay. So I ran the tags on the fuckers that were outside her place, and they belong to a Mr. Paul Gordon, the owner and manager of the solar company that chick works for." So her boss that sent her to the slums was also the asshole hunting her down. Why?

"Where have I heard that name before?" I rack my brain, trying to think of it.

"That's the thing. I nosed around and found out that he's running an underground strip club with some added benefits, and most of the chicks there ain't there of their own volition." Rage hits me full steam and I punch my wall, making a giant hole through the fucker and bloodying my knuckles up.

"I remember where I heard it. I'm gonna kill that fucker," I roar, seething like a lion ready to defend his pride.

"In time," Dom says, taking my phone from my hand and silencing any other rant with a slice of his hand across his throat. Then, he speaks directly into the phone. "Enrico, great work. Keep an eye on his operation. See who else he's working with and if I have to talk to one of the families about it." If anyone's working with that asshole, it's the Denali Family. Those assholes have been pissed since Dom put them in their place years ago.

"Yes, boss."

Dom hits the end button and tosses the phone back to me. "Where have you heard his name?"

"My informant that led me to Walsh. He said that Gordon wanted Walsh to be there to handle something. He sent Mariana there to be snatched up."

Gripping my bicep, he squeezes it and stares into my eyes. "Take a motherfucking deep breath and get your shit together. Tomorrow, you go get your girl, and then we'll deal with that fucker."

"I need her to be safe," I breathe out, letting him know where I stand.

"I understand what you're going through more than anyone. You just have to convince her that you're not as crazy as you look." He tugs on the lapel of my suit jacket with a chuckle.

"That's gonna be a hard one."

"For sure, but I'll let Aria take a crack at it if you need her." His wife would be a great help, but I don't want to overwhelm Mariana since she's probably already scared of me and who I am. Hell, she doesn't even know my name, only that I'm deadly.

"Not right away, but I need her to get supplies that women need in the house by ten in the morning."

"Okay. I'm sure my wife will be chomping at the bit when she finds out." He walks toward the door and then turns back to add, "And get some rest—you look like shit."

"Not all of us get to go home to the warmth of a good woman."

"I know." He grins from ear to ear.

Having my cousin's support reassures me that things are going to be just fine. Now all I have to do is abduct my future wife.

The night is long as I devise my plan and the way I'm to capture Mariana, although half my plan involves fucking her brains out, which only sends me on a tangent, beating off like a fucking crazed man with her panties in my hand. In fact, I think I've officially gone off the deep end.

It's well into the middle of the night, and sleep just won't come. I get up and work out, bench pressing more than my weight until I'm bone tired, and then I hit the shower. Once I land in my bed, ass naked, I pass out with dreams of Mariana filling my head.

*T*he sun's peeping through the windows like a stalker as the last bit of sleep escapes my body. I wake up with a purpose as my phone pings loudly. *Sent Tony D. to watch your prized possession. Get your lazy ass up.*

I check the time, and it's nearly ten. Fuck. I get up and dress as fast as humanly possible. Instead of my normal suit, I go with a pair of blue jeans and a black tee that hugs my muscles. I need to be ready to snatch her up easily, and a suit just won't work.

I open the door and nearly collide with Aria and Domani. "Mom's got the baby, so we're bringing these in for your woman. Get going already."

"Don't keep her from me too long," Aria says, smacking my chest.

"I'll do my best." I wink and leave them in my house. Domani has keys and can lock up after he's done.

I'm about to get in my car when Tony D sends me a message. *She's on the move. Following a bit behind.*

On my way.

He responds a moment later. *Just a block from the shelter. A local restaurant.*

Get a coffee and see what she's up to. Don't talk to her.

Understood.

I fly down there, but it takes me thirty-eight minutes. She's no longer in the restaurant, but back at the shelter. Tony and I meet outside the shelter, just away from the lot in case they're monitoring it. "Sorry. She just stayed long enough to fill out an application. She didn't grab a bite or anything."

"No. Thanks. I got this. You can do whatever else you have left."

"Cool. She's pretty, and in the wrong neighborhood."

I don't let it bother me because Tony's just stating the obvious risk. "Don't worry. I'll fix that soon."

"I'm sure you will." He smirks because it's obvious I'm a lost cause when it comes to her.

My phone rings just as Tony takes his leave. It's Dom. "What's going on?"

"I just got a call from Enrico. He says someone just pulled her tags."

"What? I'm right here, and there ain't no cops around." I have a bullet with those motherfuckers' names on them.

"Exactly. That means they're on the hunt for her. Make your move soon. I'll see who pulled it and find out who they're on the take with."

"Thanks."

"That's what family is for." Damn right. We work together to protect our family and Mariana's my family now.

I tuck away my phone after he ends the call, and I scope out the shelter.

I have to get my hands on her, and I tell myself it's to make sure she's kept her mouth shut. It's been twenty-four hours since I saw her beautiful eyes full of fear and curiosity. I want to see pleasure shining through them as I make her mine.

Suddenly and to my surprise, Mariana comes running out of the shelter in my direction. Her eyes wide and full of panic. Acting quickly, I nab her in broad daylight with my hands wrapped around her waist and my mouth closing down on hers. Her hands dig into my hair, clinging to me as I carry her to my vehicle. Realizing what we're doing, she tenses in my arms, but I continue our kiss without allowing her to break our intense first taste. Once I reach the passenger door, I finally release her mouth, and she attempts to catch her breath. Looking around, there's no one in sight so I twist her around and pin her to the vehicle, snapping the cuffs on her wrists.

"What the hell? Let me go," she cries out, wiggling and tossing her hips back.

"No, and stop fucking fidgeting. You're gonna hurt yourself."

"I wouldn't be hurting myself if you hadn't grabbed me."

I tap my finger on her nose. "You ran into my arms."

"No, I ran into a brick wall you call a chest."

"Behave." I swat her ass and set her down in the back seat.

"No," she says, fidgeting. I grip her throat which calms her down and then I put her seatbelt on. I kiss her cheek before letting go of her slender neck. Damn, my dick got rock hard at the way she reacted to my hold. I walk around to the driver's side and then slide in, locking the doors before pulling into traffic.

"Why are you doing this? I promised I wouldn't say anything." She leans forward, giving me a whiff of her scent.

"Well, that remains to be seen. Now sit back properly."

"What are you going to do with me?" A lot of fucking things... all of which will make her scream in ecstasy. The way she reacted to my kiss I know damn well we're going to be great together. Still, it's not time to mention all the fucking wicked things I want to do to her.

Keeping my cool, I answer, "Until I say otherwise, you're my captive."

"Great," she huffs, rolling her eyes and sitting back. "I'm guessing these doors don't unlock." She can't reach them without twisting awkwardly, but I made sure to put the child locks on.

"Right on that one. Now, be quiet. I need to make an

important call." I call Dom and speak in Italian, and then hang up.

"Okay. So I'm guessing you're Italian."

"You got that right. Can you speak Italian?" I didn't want her to hear what I had to say.

"No, but I understood 'Grazie.'"

"That's good because the less you know, the better." *Especially about how you'll be marrying me and having my babies as soon as I can get you naked.*

"You can trust me. I'm not going to tell anyone."

"I know you won't." A look of fear crosses her face, misunderstanding my meaning, but I'm not going to correct her just yet because I need that control until I can get her in my home where she can't escape. Call me a monster, but this isn't the worst thing I've done and technically she'll be a lot better off in my home.

I hop on the expressway and drive toward home. We live on the north side just between the border of Chicago and Arlington Heights. My estate isn't as grand as Domani's but it's nothing to sneeze at, so she'll be happy with it. Or so I hope.

She refuses to look at me directly, but every once in a while, I catch her stealing glances. "So tell me why you're at the shelter. Hiding from me?" I ask, testing her responses.

Her eyes widen in fear. I hate it, but it's a necessary evil. "No. I swear I wasn't."

"Then why were you there?" I challenge, hoping she'll tell me what's going on with those fucks.

"Um, I was getting evicted."

"In such a hurry that you left half your things? Don't lie to me, Mariana. How can I trust you if you lie to me?"

Her mouth falls open in disbelief and irritation. The irony of my question isn't lost on me. "Says the man who kidnapped me and did what you did the other day." She wags her finger, but she doesn't mention exactly what I did, which is good and bad. I don't know if she's repulsed or just keeping to her promise to stay silent on the matter.

"Well, I'm a bad man, there's no doubt, but sometimes things are necessary. So, tell me what made you speed out of your apartment like a bat out of hell if it wasn't because of me."

She looks out the window and when she looks back at the rearview mirror, her eyes are watery. "I was told if I didn't get a sale yesterday, my boss would make me earn my money another way. He just messaged saying he's found out where I am, so I ran away from the shelter."

I grip the wheel so tightly my knuckles are white, and I can almost hear the steering wheel crack under the pressure. "Don't worry about him."

"Thanks," she remarks sardonically. I want to spank her, but I'll save that for later. "I'll save all my worries for *you*."

"Don't worry about me. I'm all good." I wink at her through the rearview.

"Asshole," she mutters, glaring at me when she really wants to flip me off.

"Are you hungry? I know I get cranky when I'm hungry."

"The fuck is wrong with you? You abduct me and have the nerve to act like I don't have a right to be upset."

"Well, there's that, but I told you to relax."

She raises her eyebrows at me and then decides to ignore what I said. "How long am I your captive?"

"Until I can trust that you won't snitch." I think that should take the next seventy-years.

"Great. Well, in that case, I'm going to take a nap. It's been a rough night, and I didn't get much sleep."

"What happened? Did someone fuck with you in there?"

I snarl, hearing the leather on the wheel crack some more. Shit, I'm going to need to take my vehicle into the shop.

There goes that look of surprise on her face again. "No. Nothing happened. If you didn't notice, I had one hell of a shocking day yesterday." She gives me one final glare before closing her eyes and resting.

A few minutes later, I can tell she's fallen asleep. When we arrive at my home just down the road from Dom's, I pull through the gates and then down the path into my garage and let the large door close behind me. Still, Mariana remains asleep, so I decide to let her. She doesn't startle when I pick her up, so I carry my little captive to the bedroom across from mine.

"Rest," I whisper, placing a kiss on her temple before unlocking the cuffs. I take them with me and then walk out of the room, making sure to lock the door.

4

Mariana

I WAKE up in a bed much more comfortable than any bed I have slept on before and panic sets in, but not for the normal reason. I feared that this was a dream. From the looks of the bedroom, it wasn't.

I'm a prisoner in what looks to be a very nice home. I get out of the bed and find my bag set on the dresser. I open the drawers one by one, curious as to who the room belongs to, but they're empty. Needing to pee, I enter the en suite to find it barely stocked. Great. At least there's toilet paper and soap.

This man is seriously confusing the hell out of me. His concern sets my body aflame with lust, while he's confessing to making me his prisoner. I don't understand his motivation other than the damn fact that I saw something I shouldn't have, and he's probably worried I'll trick off to someone. I have no intention of doing anything like that because I hate dealing with the police.

When my parents died, they acted like I had something

to do with it. They fucking drove off a cliff like how could I have had something to do with it? It was a freaking accident. They bought a used RV with faulty steering and brakes. I hadn't even seen them in two months when it happened and hadn't spoken to them in over a month.

A knock at the door startles me and before I can go to it, it opens. "You're back. Do I at least get your name, or is that off limits?"

"No, I want to hear my name off your lips. It's Nero."

"Why?"

"Because that is what my parents named me."

I roll my eyes. Why do you want me to say your name?"

He smirks at me and then looks at me with that wicked stare that makes me want to climb him or onto the bed and spread my legs wide open. "Simple. I want to fuck you until you're creaming and shouting my name so loud it shakes the house."

How to I not give myself away? Arching my brow with my hands on my hips, I sneer at him and then say, "So that's why I'm here... are you going to force me?"

"Never, but enough discussing this. There's only so many times I can beat off in a day."

"You were beating off to me."

"More times than appropriate in the past twenty-four hours. Now, enough sharing. Are you hungry? You didn't eat at the restaurant, and you slept through the night."

"How did you know I went... never mind. It's probably the same way you knew where to find me."

"No, it's not exactly the same. Again, are you hungry?" My stomach answers for me with a loud rumble. "Okay. I'll take that as a yes. You can sit in here and I'll bring your food, or you can come downstairs while I finish it."

"I'll have it up here. I suppose you don't plan on returning my phone?" I challenge.

"You don't need it right now, and I can't trust you to behave, so I'll let you know when you can have it."

"I have a job, you know?" I lie.

"No you don't."

"I did until you kidnapped me."

"Liar. See, and you expect me to trust that you won't say a word." He shakes his head. "I'll have someone bring up your food. I have work to go do."

"Whatever. What am I supposed to do while you're working?"

"Watch TV, shower. One moment. He steps back to the door and grabs two large bags. "I don't know what's in here, but these are for you. I had my cousin's wife pick up the supplies you would need, and I can have a couple of books brought up for you." I like to pick my own books to read.

"No, the TV is fine." He leaves with a smirk. I listen as his footsteps fade and then I test the door. It's locked. Just like I expected—because I'm a prisoner.

I plop on the bed and grab the remote. Maybe I can find a movie to pass the time. As soon as I turn it on, *Beauty and the Beast* is playing and a rolling laugh bursts through me. Did he plan this? No. It's on the Disney Channel. A knock at the door startles me, and I jump up off the bed.

"Miss Conlon?" a man's voice calls through the door, and I can tell it's not my captor.

"Yes?" *You fucking lackey.*

"Your breakfast, ma'am."

An idea crosses my mind as I open the door to see a man in a suit. "So hello," I say with a purr, arching my back and popping my chest out to show off my large breasts.

"Ma'am, here's your food, and that's not going to work on me."

Can he tell what I'm doing? "What?"

"That flirty act. I'm not trying to die no matter how pretty you are, so please behave while Nero's out." Shit. He's on to me, and apparently Nero has all claims on his prisoner.

Scowling, I snatch the tray out of his hands like a bitch. "Fine. Get lost and lock it back up," I huff, slamming the door in his face. If that's the way they're going to treat me, I won't be grateful for the food even if it looks better than what I had planned to eat in my car. Damn it, all my snacks are going to waste. What about my car? It's not anything special, but it has all my clothes in it, and it's mine.

I'll have to ask him about getting my things. I set my food on the empty dresser and then examine what he actually gave me: a bottle of orange juice with a plate of scrambled eggs and bacon with buttered toast. What the hell? Is this the Hilton?

I snag a piece of toast between my teeth and then pull up a chair to sit near my food while watching the movie. I look at my plate and stare. "Well, aren't you going to dance?" It doesn't move. I think I got screwed in this deal. There aren't even talking dishes. I need to file a complaint.

Still, as I eat, I know one thing: this prison food is good. It's so tasty that I polish off my entire meal and feel like a glutton afterward.

———

I don't know when I passed out, but I think it was somewhere in the middle of *The Holiday* because I started dreaming of my sexy, growling captor. I wake up and find my tray gone. Scanning the room, I don't see anyone in here, but the damned sun is nearly setting. I'm trying to think of how soon the sun sets in May. Maybe six or seven? I check the TV and see it's seven-thirty.

"I need some water," I grumble.

"Coming," Nero's deep timber comes from somewhere in the room. I look, and there's an intercom on the nightstand. That wasn't there earlier. What the hell?

A minute later, my cell door is opened by the sexy brute in just a plain white dress shirt with the sleeves rolled up his forearms, revealing a tattoo on each arm. Fuck, could he be any hotter? I hate him so damned much.

Okay, I don't hate him.

I *do* hate him. What am I thinking? He kidnapped me, but I am in a better situation than I was.

"Here you go." He hands me the water and turns on his heel, only to stop at the open door. "I'm cooking dinner. Do you want to come out now, or would you like to keep up this petulant attitude?"

"Petulant? You fucking kidnapped me, you asshole," I shout, crossing my arms.

"Okay, I guess that's my answer. Dinner will be brought up," he says with a shrug, closing the door.

I jump off the bed and call out before he can finish closing it. "Wait. You cook?"

He steps back in the room and cracks a killer smile that nearly has me on my ass or my knees. What the hell is going on with my libido? Did they spike my food? "Not all the time, but since it's just the two of us in here, someone had to cook."

"It's just you and me?" I question. Where are his servants that took care of my food today? Hell, I didn't even touch the lunch the one dude brought up because I was too sleepy from the breakfast that I inhaled to do more than take a bite of my sandwich.

He crosses the distance, closing in to within a foot of me. Arching his brow, he warns, "Yes, but don't think of running. I'll catch you and bend you over, spanking that cute ass of yours." I try to hide the lust circling my nervous system.

"Fine. Lead me to the food. I'm starving."

"Wow, was that so hard?" he questions, like I don't have a reason to be upset by this whole thing.

"Not as hard as your head," I mutter, following behind him. The other guy isn't there anymore, so we must really be alone. My pulse picks up a couple of notches.

"Either one of them," he says with a chuckle, which resonates through me as if he's strumming my clit like a guitar. Why am I attracted to a killer?

"So what is it that you do?" I ask, changing the subject and not taking the bait. After all, this place is a mansion and since I witnessed him take someone out... or did I? Now that I think about it, he wasn't there when I woke up. No. He was most certainly dead.

"What I do?" he repeats as he turns and looks back at me as we walk through the entryway down to another corridor. I see the front door, but I ignore the urge to even take a more sparing glance. I reason that I can't escape before he catches me.

"I'm the second-in-command for the Bianchi family."

"Second-in-command? So you take orders from someone else? Don't you want to be... what do you call it? The Don?"

He spins on his heel, glaring down at me like I hit a sore spot. Gripping me around my biceps without squeezing hard, he clears his throat and says, "No. Not now, not ever. That spot belongs to my cousin, and I'd never do anything to hurt him or his family. Why? Does that bother you that I don't run his empire?"

"No. Just testing your loyalty."

"And did I pass?"

"It's not a pass or fail."

We finally reach a large double-door entryway and he opens it, stepping in first. "Well, come on through here and don't think about the knives. I'd hate for you to cut yourself."

Snapping my fingers at the missed opportunity, I sneer and remark, "Damn, you're on top of it. Do you normally kidnap people?"

There's a smug expression on his chiseled face that turns to lust in those penetrative eyes. "Not normally, but I never bring them home." I blush, knowing he wants to fuck me. I'm starting to believe that's the only reason he hasn't offed me.

"So what are you making?" I ask, taking a seat on a stool in front of the kitchen island, which is full of food being prepped.

"I'm making homemade ravioli," he says as he slips on an apron. How is that even sexy? It's a light gray one that says *Great Cooks are Italian.* A pang of jealousy hits me as I consider who bought that for him, which is crazy because I'm his prisoner. I've got Stockholm Syndrome seeping into my brain, making its home there. I'm betting it's because of the movie and has nothing to do with the fact that he's gorgeous and my life here is better than where it was heading.

"Wow, and you said you don't cook often, but you got a fancy apron?"

"Well, I am Italian, and my zia bought it for me for Christmas." I watch him as he rubs an egg wash over the puffy pasta.

"Sorry—zia?"

"Yes, it means aunt."

"Oh. Yeah, sorry. I'm Irish and whatever mix my parents had." He's listening while pressing the fork to the pasta, sealing it closed in a smooth flowing pace. "You make it look easy."

"The trick is practice. Would you like something to drink?" he asks, taking a drink from a glass with red wine in it.

"I'm not old enough to drink." He ducks his head, scowling at me. "Okay, so you're not above breaking the law."

"I do have non-alcoholic drinks, but with the food, I do have the perfect wine."

"Juice would be good. I need something other than water." He turns around and goes to the fridge. I think about running, but my feet remain planted. I should dash as fast as I can away from here, and yet here I am, sitting like a good girl. *It's not like I know where I am or how to get out of here before he could find me*, I keep reasoning to myself.

"We have apple or orange juice."

"I'll take apple." I had orange juice for breakfast. He pours a glass and then hands it to me. Our fingers touch, and a little gasp passes my lips with a pleasurable shock. Nero quickly takes his hand away and goes back to cooking as if he didn't feel that, but his hand is a little unsteady on the last of the raviolis.

His phone rings, and he sets everything down to answer it. "Hello, Aria." That's all I get because he goes into speaking Italian to her, which pisses me off. I get out of my seat, feeling an insane amount of jealousy. He ends the call just as I make it to the kitchen door and is on me before I get two more steps. Nero's thick, muscular arms wrap around my waist and he spins me to face the wall outside the kitchen.

"Nice try," he growls in my ear as his body presses into my back. "You're a very bad girl. Just when I thought things were going well. I hope you got enough to drink because it's time to go back to your room."

"Why—are you worried your girlfriend will find me here?"

A deep, rumbling laugh rips through him. "I don't have a wife or a girlfriend or anyone. That woman I was talking to is Dom's wife, Aria. She wants to hang out with you, but I can't trust you to behave and Domani won't let you hurt his wife."

"Why would she want to hang out with me?"

"Because you're close in age, and she only has her son to hang out with most days unless her family stops by."

"Oh—I don't want to go back to my room yet."

"I'm only going to give you one more chance." His tongue dips out, licking my pulse while his cock grinds against my ass. I can't bite back the moan as pleasure floods my pussy. "Don't try that shit again, or I'll forget my manners." He nips at my ear, then pulls away and leads me into the kitchen.

I sit back in my chair and don't say another word. My face is hot from both embarrassment and his touch. "So you're barely nineteen. Where are your parents?"

"They died."

"I'm sorry. When was this?"

"A year ago. What about yours?"

"My father was a piece of shit and died years ago. My mother lives in Italy, and we haven't spoken in twenty years and she's no better."

"Wow. That's rough. I thought most boys loved their mothers."

"My aunt is like a mother to me. When I turned seven, my mother didn't want anything to do with my father and me. She fled to Italy and married someone else. For years, I thought my father had killed her and lied to me, but then I saw her with her husband when I went to Italy for a vacation. She looked at me with disgust and then walked away with her nose in the air."

"Why? Does she know what you do?"

"Oh yes. She left because my father wasn't the Don and I wouldn't be in charge. She wanted to be the queen of it all."

"Oh shit. My bad about the whole joke earlier."

"It's fine. If I didn't know better, I'd say you knew all about me and how to stick it right to me."

"So why did you hate your father?"

"Well, he wanted the same thing for me and for himself, but he was a coward and didn't pull off the coup he wanted. Instead, he got a bullet."

"Oh shit. I don't understand how people you're close to can be so terrible." I choke on my own tears as I think about my parents' sudden dismissal of me. They changed after my father's heart attack, and they were never the same with me.

"Don't cry, baby." I feel his hand wiping away my tears.

"Sorry." Our eyes lock and I feel the pull, but then my phone rings, and it's not in my pocket. It's in his.

"Hello?" he answers, keeping his eyes focused on me. "Never mind who the hell this is. Who the fuck are you to call my woman's phone? CPD, you say? Your name and badge number. It sure as fuck matters to me." He grabs his phone and types something in it before responding to the man on the other end. "Missing? She's not missing. Who reported her missing? Her fiancé?" He stiffens and then relaxes. "Well, that's nuts because she doesn't have one. Have a good day. Don't call again." He ends the call and tosses it on the counter. "Fiancé?"

"I don't have a fiancé. I don't even have a boyfriend."

He stares at me with determination in his eyes. "That's really good because I'd have to add another dead body to my count this week."

"How many do you have this week?"

"Only the fuck you saw." He continues working on dinner, dropping the ravioli into a boiling pot like it's not a big deal. Hell, I'm not even acting like it's an issue.

"Who was that on the phone?"

"It was the police," he says with his broad, muscular back to me.

"I swear I didn't," I exclaim.

He turns around with a ladle in his hand. "Relax. I know you didn't. See—I'm not the only one keeping tabs on you." He goes back to working on the food as if that's not pertinent information.

"What?" I screech, throwing my hands up and nearly sending my juice flying.

"Don't worry about it. Like I told you, everything is going to be just fine."

"Excuse me, but I'm just supposed to trust you?"

He has two plates set with a layer of sauce and topped with ravioli's and some sort of seasoning on top. Setting them down in front of us, he says, "I wouldn't let anyone touch a hair on your head, so yes. Come, dinner's almost ready."

"You are a confusing man."

"Well, let's just say you confuse me in ways I didn't know were possible. Let's sit at the table." There's a small kitchen table in the corner that I hadn't noticed since I refused to take my eyes off Nero.

"Do you want me to carry anything?" I ask, trying to at least help. I've never been a lazy ass no matter how tired I was.

"If you'd like, you can take the salad to the table."

We sit down with a beautiful salad, pasta, and wine. I forget all about the juice because I've always wondered what made wine good with food. "You went all out for dinner."

"I like to eat. Now dig in." I nod and just dive into my ravioli. It's freaking incredible, which takes me by surprise. I don't know why it does, since I watched him make them and he appeared to be a professional at it.

"What the hell?" he scowls, setting his fork on the table and then pulling his phone out of his pocket.

He disappears for ten minutes and when he comes back, he's scowling. "Sorry about that. It seems we have another matter that I have to deal with. Eat, so I can get out of here."

"I'm done." I push away my plate, hating the suddenly icy demeanor.

"You've had two bites. You don't like it?"

"It's fine, and I've had four raviolis and at least a quarter of my salad since you left. I'm actually quite full. I have a small stomach as of late."

"Why is that?"

"Did you not see me living in a hovel and then in a shelter? I'm not sitting on a pile of cash."

"Sorry about that."

"Don't be. It's not your problem. Can I just go up to my room?" A feeling of defeat washes over me, not that I'd let him see it. I keep my shoulders taut and my chin up with a little more attitude than necessary.

"Yes. I'll walk you up."

"Yes, you don't want me escaping."

It's supposed to come out snide, but all he does is nod and say, "Damn right. You wouldn't get far because we're extremely isolated."

I'm not sure why I'm being a bitch other than I'm a prisoner and he just reminded me of it, even though I felt something simmering between us. Maybe that's just how he operates with women. Hot and cold, or maybe it's the fact that I'm not here on my own volition. There's nothing between us, and I need to remember that. I'm nothing more than a means to an end. A repair of a mistake.

"Whatever. Listen, dinner was nice, but from now on, please bring my slice of bread and water to my cell, please."

"Since you asked so nicely," he snarls, not saying a word again as he closes the door behind me.

5

Nero

FUCK. I don't know what happened right now, but I can't deal with it. Apparently, Gordon isn't taking no for an answer, and the slippery fuck has insiders in the police department so he's got a little pull. I lock the door and look right at Tony D. "If anything happens to her, I'll string you up by your balls. Do I make myself clear?" I trust him, but when it comes to my future wife, he better be ready to lay down his life for her.

"Of course, Nero. She's to be protected at all costs," he answers, understanding the depths of my intentions. Mariana is the be-all and end-all of my happiness.

"Good." I steal a look back at the stairs, aching to run up there and apologize for whatever I did to hurt that fragile connection we have. Still, I have business to deal with and the sooner it's dealt with, the better it will be for everyone. I jump in my truck and drive straight to Dom's where he's waiting for me as soon as I walk through the door.

"Hey. Let's talk in the kitchen. You look like shit, by the way."

I nod and follow behind him. "Thanks. I feel like it."

"Is she fighting you?" he questions, smiling widely at me. He loves when Aria gives him lip.

"I don't know. We were having a good moment and then I left to take the call regarding Gordon and all the information Enrico and Vinnie pulled. When I came back, she'd gone back to reminding me how she's a prisoner."

"Did you kiss her? It helps when they get moody," he offers up his advice as a married man.

"Oh really?" Aria says, stepping into the room with her arms crossed and brow raised.

Dom pales and stammers out, "That's not what I meant." He's the man people cower down to when he enters a room, but she has that power over him that only she can possess.

"Bullshit, Domani. Own it. Anyway, I'm moody and yes, your kisses help because I love you. They are just meeting. It might take a while for her to tolerate his shit. So what did you say when you said you had to leave?" She has one hand on her hip and the other is pointing a finger at me.

"I said to hurry up and eat because I had to leave." I run my hands through my hair because as the words leave my mouth I know why she's pissed.

"Well, fuck. I could have told you that was stupid," Domani says, shaking his head.

"My wise, all-knowing key to women is right. You were essentially dismissing her from your presence, so no wonder she iced you out."

"What the fuck am I supposed to do? I don't trust that she won't leave if I let her and yet, I know it's fucking wrong to hold her captive like that."

"Tomorrow I'll be going over there." She puts her hand

on Dom's mouth, silencing any objection he was going to toss out. "I am. She needs some girl time to discuss what an asshat you are."

"How is bashing me going to help?"

"Oh, feeble man. You can butcher men, get in their heads before you kill them, but you can't figure out something so simple."

"Simple? Ha. Women—simple?" Dom barks out, chuckling.

"I'd choose your next words wisely, husband."

"I love you, my queen." He winks at me as he kisses her cheek, but she's wise to him and slaps his chest.

"Nice try. Now, I'll let you guys talk shop, but I'm deadly serious about tomorrow. Someone's got to save your dumbass from making a fool of yourself." She kisses Dom's cheek and leaves the room after stealing my piece of cake. Strangely, my stomach hurts too much to care.

"I'll cut you another slice."

"I'm good. Let's deal with this prick. So he's a huge cokehead, but that's nothing. He operates a strip club and there are hookers running around. Many of them are reportedly not there voluntarily."

"Are you serious?"

"Deadly. The fucker needs to go down. I went to her apartment last night and the shit had been turned inside out. The place was completely ransacked."

"So we deal with him, but we need to be careful. He's kept out of trouble with his hands in these pots because he more than likely has people on the take, and I'm not just talking about the police; maybe a councilman or two who turn their heads, officials from other states. It could be anyone."

"He's hell-bent on getting a hold of Mariana. I refuse to let that happen, but I'm gonna need help."

"Of course. You're like my brother. We're blood, and if you truly believe she's the one, then I got your back."

I frown and tilt my head before asking a question I already know the answer to. "How long did it take you to decide Aria was yours?"

"One look."

"Exactly."

He nods, confirming my answer and respecting it. "We'll go to war with Gordon, but I'd prefer if we just got rid of the problem from behind the scenes. The less mess and attention for us, the better."

"I agree. His club is just between the two Southside families on the outskirts of the city, so there's a chance that they're backing him."

"I'll contact them and see what they know about that little bitch and how much they want to dismantle his shitty club."

"Thanks."

"No problem. The only problem is when the girls team up against us."

"Thank fuck you had a boy and have another on the way."

"Damn right. Now go home and we'll handle this shit first thing in the morning. I'll send Aria over for a breakfast chit-chat while we deal with business. With her guards and a few extra, both ladies will be safe."

I nod, and we hug before parting ways. The second I'm in my truck, I feel a fuck ton better knowing that Domani has my back. A huge part of me already knew that, but there's something powerful about hearing it from his mouth. I drive back to the house with a feeling of comfort.

Entering my property, I quietly climb the stairs and notice that her bedroom light is off.

"Good. Tomorrow, we'll have a fresh start," I say, walking to my room.

I slept like shit. She was right across the hall, sleeping like an angel, and all I could think about was touching her until she caved to me. If only I can get her to see we're meant to be together because once I do, she'll have my baby inside of her. That way, she'll have a hard time leaving me.

It's just seven in the morning and Aria has already texted me, letting me know I have an hour to get my ass ready to meet with Domani because she and Luca will be here soon. I roll my eyes, but I get up and head over to Mariana's room. Unlocking the door, I open it to find her working out, throwing punches in the air. God, her ass looks so damn good in those itty-bitty shorts. Her punches need work, but the venom in the strikes lets me know she's readying herself for a showdown.

"Are those for me?" I ask. She spins around and her mouth falls open. Fuck, I forgot I'm just wearing a pair of boxers.

"Is that for me?" she asks, staring at my unmistakable erection which takes the opportunity to jerk under her perusal as if he's nodding yes. "Is there something you wanted?"

"There's a lot I want. Especially when it comes to that smart mouth of yours."

"Oh yeah? Well, excuse me, I need to shower." She turns her back to me and lifts the hem of her top over her head and tosses it on the floor. I close the distance, grabbing her around the waist and carrying her to the bed. With her bare breasts between us, I slam my mouth onto hers, letting her pebbled nipples brush across my chest.

Her hands dig into the muscles of my shoulders, scoring my skin as she rolls her hips up against my throbbing need. I trail kisses down the column of her throat, nipping and sucking on her smooth flesh, aching for so much more. "Nero," she moans, and I nearly shoot off my load in my boxers.

"Mariana, you're driving me insane. I need you to come for me. I want to hear your cries as you explode." The blunt head of my cock presses into her entrance, our clothes the only thing keeping me from penetrating her when it's all I want. I dip down and kiss a path to her tits while she grips and claws from my scalp down to my back. Our movements are frantic and intense. All new to me, and I'm doing my best to not jet my load all over the inside of my boxers. "Damn it, amore. Come for me."

She lets out a whimpering moan that grows as her body shatters, and then her moans shift to a wild cry of my name. Her orgasm is a fucking sight to behold, and luckily I'm the only one to witness it. I kiss her as she comes down, allowing my jealousy of other men to keep me from nutting just yet.

Cupping her chin, I look into her unbelievably gray eyes and confess, "I can't wait to taste your cream all over my tongue. You're a goddess when you let go."

"I can't believe it. I mean, I... I just. Wow. I don't know why I let you do that to me."

"You taunted a bull and waved the flag in my face. You're lucky I didn't pierce you like I wanted to. Now that I've experienced how sexy you are when you come, I need you to get ready."

"You're letting me leave?"

"No, but Aria's coming over here with Luca."

"What?"

"Yeah. I tried to tell her that it wasn't okay, but she listens to no one. Hell, Dom will kill a bastard if he talks back to him, but Aria is the one to make him crumble."

"Well, then, since I'm not going to get out of it, please leave me so I can shower."

"With pleasure." I stand and my cock juts out, stretching the material. I do my best to adjust him and then walk out of the room with a hint of dignity. Now, it's time to beat off. I don't know how Dom made it three years waiting for Aria. It's insane how much I want Mariana.

6

Mariana

I WATCH him walk out of the room with his cock so big and long. A part of me feels upset that he didn't come like I did. I guess with experience comes a level of control. Still, I'm thoroughly relaxed. I can barely catch my breath as I toss my head back on the bed. I'm not ready to shower, but I don't have a choice because we'll have company soon. Does she know I've been kidnapped? Maybe she was too.

Shaking my head, I try to ignore any interest in any future with Nero. He's an underboss of a mafia family, and he's actually killed someone in front of me. Why doesn't that bother me like it should? From the first time our eyes locked, I could only focus on wanting his mouth on mine. Now that I have, nothing else matters other than getting extra kisses and so much more.

After getting out of the shower, I select a pair of jean shorts and a tank top. It's almost the end of Spring and quite a warm day. I sit on the bed and wait for Nero to unlock the door, but when the knob turns, it's not him, but a beautiful raven-haired woman with a baby in her arms.

"Hi. Sorry to barge in on you like this, but Luca and I needed some time away from the guys, and my sister has abandoned me for Ireland. Like what the heck does Ireland have that I don't? Oh, I guess I should introduce myself. I'm Aria Bianchi, and I'm Dom's wife. I don't know if you know who he is, but anyways, Dom and Nero are cousins. So I came to welcome you to the family."

"Welcome me to the family?"

"Yeah. Pretty soon you'll be a Bianchi as well."

"Did Nero tell you that I'm his girlfriend or something, because that's not..."

"Please. I know exactly what you're doing here. He's an idiot. A kind-hearted killer, but he's a man with very few brain cells when it comes to women. So anyways, this little guy is my sweet Luca, and we're gonna have some breakfast together. Now that you're dressed, how about we head downstairs? I brought my chef, Giuseppe, with me. You'll love him. Although don't let Nero hear that. They get really possessive when you mention love, but Giuseppe's food is to die for. Come." She stands with the baby and walks to the door. "Well, are you coming?"

I like her. She seems a bit over the top, but she's nothing like I expected. We head downstairs and there's a handsome man standing at the bottom, scowling at Aria. He looks so much like Nero that it's shocking, and then he pulls Aria into his arms for a kiss. "What did I say about going up and down the stairs with the baby?"

"He's not heavy, Domani."

"I don't care. You're pregnant. Get your pretty ass in the kitchen and eat. I'm going to take my little boy with us to talk shop." Does he mean they're talking about killing more people? He nods at me without a word and takes the boy with him as if he read my mind. Fuck, did I say that aloud?

"Ugh. That man thinks I need to be on bedrest when I'm pregnant. Anyway, let's eat. I'm starving." She takes my hand and leads me into the kitchen.

"Did he kidnap you too?" I ask Aria, wondering if that's how they get their women. Fucking cavemen.

A man with a chef's uniform starts laughing as he comes out of the pantry. Oops—I hadn't seen him there. "Giuseppe, this is Mariana. She's new to our world," she says with a wink.

He sets down the ingredients that were in his arms onto the counter in front of us. "It's a pleasure to meet such a lovely creature. Now, what can I make you for breakfast?"

"You don't have to."

"Ah, very charming, but you're too modest. How about some pancakes and sausage?" he insists and frankly it sounds too good to pass up.

"That's fine."

"So, anyway. I wasn't kidnapped. I was promised to my husband."

"They still do things like that?" I know that I'm being rude, but I thought women had backbones—like I'm one to talk.

She giggles and then takes a drink of juice that her chef set down for her. "Yes and no. Honestly, I'm not complaining. I was at first, but I'd already had a crush on the big goon before I learned of our engagement."

"So you weren't mad at your parents?" I'd tell them to fuck off and run away.

"Hell, yes, I was. I was afraid to marry him because I

thought he believed I was nothing but a piece of property. Honestly, I couldn't resist him. Anyway, it wasn't long before I learned that my husband was obsessed with me and had asked for my hand two years before we got married. Crazy, right?"

"Very." And yet, I want to know more about their relationship.

"So here we are. Happily married and with a small and ever-growing family." She rubs her baby bump, grinning from ear to ear which makes me sad.

I'm not here because Nero's madly in love with me. "What does it matter? I'm just a liability. I saw something I shouldn't have, so he took me captive."

"Yes, you did, but that's not why he brought you here. He'd already decided to let you go, and then he couldn't stay away. It has nothing to do with what you saw. Nero doesn't believe you'll snitch on him, but he needs an excuse to keep you close to him."

"Are you serious?" I wonder if she's right about that.

Giuseppe nods while Aria continues. "I'm telling you that's the truth. He's a fool, but the man is a little crazy about you."

She makes a good case for Nero. I sigh. "I guess that would explain some of his behavior, but he blows from hot to cold." Like last night and then this morning where he made me come for him.

"Ah, is this about dinner last night?" she asks, taking a drink of her orange juice.

"Damn, you know everything," I huff.

She pats my hand and tilts her head to get my attention. I meet her gaze, and she says, "Look, I love Nero like a brother, and that means making sure he's happy and healthy. The man has a sweet tooth, just so you know.

Anyway, I listened in and gave him my two cents, for what it's worth. He was a bit stressed out and didn't mean to come off as harsh or dismissive. They had important things to discuss, and time was of the essence." She takes a drink of her orange juice before adding. "He's afraid if he gives you free rein, you'll run away from him."

Ugh. I suppose he does have a reason to be concerned about me fleeing, although my feet don't want to rush to the door. Instead, I keep myself planted, relaxed, and strangely anxious for his return. The way he made me come is insane, and my body craves a repeat performance with every second that passes.

"Oh." I don't have an answer to all her revelations, but thankfully, Giuseppe is not only a masterful chef, but he's also quick and he sets our plates in front of us.

"This looks and smells fantastic," I confess as I grab the syrup and coat my pancakes. I'm hungrier than I thought.

"It really is. I swear you have no idea. This man is a magician." She pats Giuseppe's hand.

He smiles and says, "I'll clean up while you ladies enjoy."

"Let's take this in the dining room." We're about to go into the dining room when a man comes up to us.

"Signora Bianchi?"

"Yes, Luigi?"

"The boss said to give you these." He hands her a stack of mail.

"Oh, goodness, this is a lot. Thank you, Luigi." She takes the letters and smiles. "I guess Ireland is fabulous for my sister."

I wonder if her sister is just like her, beautiful and energetic. "Is she there alone?"

"No, she's with her husband and children. I personally

had a bad experience over there and don't care for it that much, although it's absolutely gorgeous."

"I've never been." There's so much more to that story and I want to know more but I won't press.

"Well, one day you can make Nero take you. He hardly ever takes a day off, but I'm sure he'll make time for you."

"I think you got our relationship twisted. The man kidnapped me."

She scoffs. "And you're upset that he dismissed you last night at dinner, right?" I can't reply because any denial out of my mouth would be a bald-faced lie. "See? You're attracted to him, despite everything. Just go with the flow. The man needs you to be his anchor. Can you be the reason he loves to come home?"

"What about what I need?" I want to kick myself for letting my emotions show, so I take a bite of my sausage.

"And what is that?" she challenges.

"Someone who won't abandon me when things get hard." I've had enough abandonment issues that I don't believe I could handle more.

"Oh, so last night..."

"I didn't realize how bothered I'd been about it, but I couldn't sleep all night." Nero's definitely more to me that my captor and I knew that from the moment he held me in his arms after I fainted. The kiss outside the women's shelter only proved it some more, but last night was the icing on the cake. Nero could break me.

"Trust me when I say he's not going anywhere."

"What about having other lovers?"

"That's a hard fucking no," Nero growls. For a man his size, he moves with such stealth and agility. He stalks toward me, sliding his hand to the back of my neck and tilting my head so our faces are an inch apart. "Don't ever think I'd allow another man to take my place." He kisses me hard and fierce, a connection so profound it's filled with possession.

When Nero pulls away, I'm panting and Aria says, "Idiot, she's talking about you banging other chicks."

"No one, and I mean no one, will ever take your place." He kisses me again, and this time it's so tender that I nearly melt in my seat. I cling to the lapels of his suit jacket.

"Um... I think it's time I go before you two start screwing at the table. Come on, Giuseppe. Let's give them some privacy."

As soon as they leave the kitchen, Nero whispers, "So where were we?"

"Apparently about to screw on the counter," I toss out there, hoping he might be willing to take the bait.

"No. The day I make you mine, it'll be in our bed."

"I don't want to be your prisoner anymore."

"I'm never letting you go, Mariana." Immediately those words shoot straight to my heart and crush all my hopes. I shove him away. Tears well up in my eyes, knowing I'm nothing more to him.

He wipes my tears and says, "Is it really so bad to be with me?"

"I can't be your captive forever."

"I'm your captive, Mariana. Whether you know it or not, you're all I think about. I should have stayed on task that day and you wouldn't have seen the ugly side of my life, but as I was driving around, I spotted you an hour earlier. All thoughts were on finding you instead of what Dom sent me to handle. I lost control of the situation because I wanted to hunt you down. I went about it the wrong way, but I'm fucking obsessed with you."

"Then what are we doing?" I ask. I'm so confused.

"We're gonna start all over. I'm Nero Bianchi, second-in-command of the Bianchi Family and all of its businesses. And you are, angel face?"

"I'm Mariana Conlon, I'm unemployed, and I obey every law."

He smiles down at me and asks, "How about you have dinner with me tonight?"

"Really? Outside?" I'm bouncing in my chair at the idea of us being a real couple.

"Not just yet, but not because I don't trust you, angel face. We're having some problems, and it's not safe." Now that's something I can understand given how we met.

"Can I cook dinner?" I ask.

"If you'd like, but I'd rather you relaxed. How about you finish your pancakes, and we spend the afternoon watching a movie and making out?"

"I've never done that before," I confess, ducking my head with embarrassment.

He tips my chin with his fingers, and I meet his gaze. "That's really good because I'd have to find all those little punks and fuck them up." The look on his face is serious as hell.

"Can you give me a kiss now?" I ask, needing his sexy, talented mouth on mine, devouring me.

"I'll give all the kisses you want." His mouth is on mine, slipping his tongue past my lips, playing with mine. He pulls back just enough to attack my ear with his lips and teeth. "I'll kiss you anywhere you want."

"So on the sofa, the bed..."

"Brat. I meant I'm going to kiss your large, sexy breasts all the way down until I'm kissing your mound, licking and sucking on your pussy." I shiver with need, closing my legs around his thighs.

"That sounds so good."

With a growl, he kisses me again and says, "Too good. Eat your breakfast, and I'll be nice and make you come."

"It's not nice to make me wait."

"Who said anything about making you wait?" He lifts me off the chair, taking a seat there and sitting me on his lap so I'm facing my food. Nero's fingers flick open the button on my shorts before deftly sliding his hand under my panties until he cups my kitten. I moan, rolling my hips to get more of his hand between my legs. "Eat before I do."

"You want a bite?" I offer my fork with a piece of pancake on it.

"Of you. Now eat your food, or I'll stop."

"Please don't," I beg.

"Then be a good girl for me." Every word from his mouth sends pleasure over my entire body. I don't know how he expects me to eat this way, but I'll do my best while he gives me his best.

"Yes, sir." I take a bite and chew before he slips a finger through my wet lips.

"So sticky, and I bet it's so damn sweet. I can't wait to have your cunt on my tongue," he whispers along the shell of my ear. He sucks my earlobe between his teeth and then takes a gentle nibble.

"Nero, oh my goodness." I clench my legs together, nearly sliding off his body, searching for relief.

"Eat," he commands.

"Yes. Fuck, yes. Okay." I take another bite while he strokes my clit, and pumps one finger into my soaked pussy. His other hand slips under my top and bra, cupping my tits and giving them a rough squeeze. With a pluck of my hardened nipple, I nearly buck off the seat as my orgasm hits me hard. Shaking and clenching around his finger, I hump his hand.

"There you go. Ride my fingers, rock that ass on my cock. I can't wait to come inside your tight little pussy." His gruff, deep voice gives me that little push to send me over the edge.

"Fuck, Nerrooo," I stammer, riding the wave of my orgasm and using him to get me off.

"That's it. Now. Finish your food." He pulls his hand free, bringing it to his lips and sucking off all my juices. "Damn, I'm gonna need to have you on my tongue soon. Eat now, please."

"What about you?" I ask, knowing his dick is rock hard, considering I was rubbing it along my ass with each flex of my hips.

"I plan to eat—very, very soon."

I mean this. I reach out and stroke the massive package that's ready to burst from his black slacks. "This isn't about me. It's about showing my woman that I can make her happy."

"What if it makes me happy to make you happy?" I offer. His eyes darken with desire, sending my pulse racing. Lust shoots through my veins even though I just came on his hand and I have a feeling that being this close to him will always drive me into a frenzied, horny state.

"Baby, you have no idea how you already do that, but if it makes you happy to see the power you have, be my guest. I'll fucking take whatever you want to give me."

With an arch of my brow, I slide off my chair and drop to my knees, grabbing his belt and freeing it from the loop. I unclasp his pants and tug on his zipper, which nearly gives way. Nero's cock jerks under his boxer briefs.

Yanking the material down, I let his massive length out to play.

"Sit." He does as I command. I've never done this before, but I think I can figure it out.

"Don't tease me, amore. Suck it," he growls, running his fingers down my cheek.

"Like this?" I ask softly before sliding it into my mouth a few inches and feeling his body flex under my fingers as I use his thighs for leverage.

"Yes," he hisses through his teeth, clenching his fists at his sides. Popping my mouth off, I lick from the base to the tip before greedily sucking on the fat head. Shit. My pussy floods again, aching for more. Sucking harder and faster, I push down deeper, nearly taking him all the way in before gagging and letting off. His fingers move to my head, sprawling out around the back of my skull; he's itching to fuck my face. I can feel he's holding back, but I'm ready for this. I want him to show me how to please him.

I release his cock. "I didn't say you were finished."

"Neither did I," I sass, grazing my teeth along the tip. Tremors run through him as he grips my hair. "Take what you want. I'm yours."

"Damn right you are. Now, suck good because I want you to choke on my cock," he growls, pulling my hair just hard enough to sting, but nothing painful. I take him down deep and then he takes over, pumping his hips up until my nose brushes against his pubis and his cock sits in my throat. "Fuck, baby, you're so good. I'm gonna come. Pull off, or I'm gonna nut." I suck hard and he unleashes his lust-filled orgasm, roaring as he shoots his load. It's so far back I hardly taste him as he coats my throat.

Finally he lets go and I pull back, resting my head on his thigh. Nero scoops me up and holds me in his arms. "I think you're trying to kill me," he grunts, his heart racing out of control.

I lift my head up and look up at him with disbelief. "I believe you were the one choking me."

His face floods with concern. "I hope I wasn't too rough with you. I just lost control."

"It was so good. I wasn't bad for a first timer?"

His eyes shoot open with a look of genuine surprise. I guess I did a good job. "You could have fooled me, angel face."

"I need a nap now," I mutter as we sit on a kitchen chair, clothes disheveled and half off.

"Let me take you to bed, and then we can watch a movie later." He kisses my lips softly and I want more, but I'm too tired to push it.

"Okay." He stands up and sets me on my feet. Then he tucks his cock back into his boxers before pulling up his pants and zippering them closed.

"Let's go." Lifting me up into his arms, cradling me, he carries me back to my room. A hint of sadness overcomes me, but I mask it before he can look down and read my expression.

"I'm going to handle some business. It's going to be a little while."

"It's fine. I'll be sleeping." I give him an exaggerated yawn and roll onto my side with my hands under my head and my knees bent.

"Rest, angel face." He presses his lips to my temple and then leaves. This time, I don't hear the latch on the door. My heart does a flip in my chest as I smile to myself. I might not be sleeping in his bed, but he trusts me enough to leave the door unlocked. I turn onto my back and look up at the ceiling.

Where does this go from here? I feel like I jumped the gun on this relationship. I've done things I've never done with anyone. I had a boyfriend in high school, but we only kissed and never the way Nero kisses me. His kisses are loaded with intent, passion, and hunger. I can't even remember my ex's kisses.

"I think I'm in love with a killer."

No. I know it. I love the devil's henchman.

7

Nero

SHE'S PISSED that I haven't fucked her yet. I'm pissed at myself for letting the teasing go so far when she's not my wife just yet. It's been three days of pure torment since that moment in the kitchen when I brought her to orgasm with my fingers and she sucked me off. Hell, I haven't gotten that image of her down on her knees out of my head, and every night I beat off to that vision. I've kissed her a lot since then but work always gets in the way of much more. I want her to ride my face and cock until I fill her with my seed and then she can't leave me.

Rubbing my hand over my face, I think about my sweet sleeping beauty upstairs. It's still quite early and I have a lot to tackle, but all I long to do is rush upstairs and take what's mine. My doorbell rings, and Tony answers it.

"Nero, Signore Bianchi is here to see you." I walk around the desk and step out in the hall to greet my zio.

"Zio, what brings you to see me?" We briefly hug, and I lead him to my office so we can speak privately.

Like Domani's, my office is completely soundproof. He arches his brow at me with a smirk. I've kept Mariana and our situation from them because I know what I'm doing isn't right, even though I don't know how to smooth things out completely between Mariana and me.

"What's this, you have a girl and you haven't introduced us to her. Your zia is quite put out with you." He wags his finger at me, which means he's been sent here by the boss herself and she's displeased.

"I want to, but our relationship is complicated," I sigh. The reality of the situation is I'm so out of my depths that I don't know how to fix it.

"Have you and her…" I promised him I wouldn't, but I'm not sure I can resist forever.

"Not yet."

"But you keep her in your home." He raises that brow again, questioning my actions. Hell, I question it as well, but my mind is made up. Mariana is mine.

"That's because she will be my wife soon."

"Well, I don't want to tell you how to live your life, but hiding her away from the family like a dirty secret isn't good."

"I'm not hiding her away. Didn't Dom tell you that I kidnapped her?"

"Oh. No, he didn't. So it's like that. Good," he says, nodding with a grin.

"I thought you'd be angry."

"Ah, sometimes it's the only way they can see it's where they belong." He winks and then gives me a hug. "Take care. We want to meet her before you two marry, at least."

"How did Domani wait so long?"

"Because he knew he couldn't touch her, so he kept his

distance. Your queen is in your home—temptation at your fingertips."

Domani calls just as I walk my uncle to the door. "I know I said you could have the day off, but I think it's time to move on Gordon."

"Have you gotten the latest report?"

"Yes. Come over."

"On my way."

"Ah, zio, it looks like I'm headed over."

"And what about your beauty locked away? She doesn't have dancing dishes to talk to, does she?" It's not lost on me that I'm a beast.

"But I do have a great library for her to slide across like Belle."

"I told you it was a good idea." He winks and steps out. I write a note on the door and then leave the house. I should go in and see her, but since I left her sleeping, I don't want to wake her.

When I get over to Dom's house, my zia is waiting to slap my arm. "I'm sorry. I'll bring her soon."

"Yeah, they have a lot more to work out than Domani and I did. Shit, our troubles look like a cakewalk," Aria says, coming into the room with the baby in her arms.

"Amore, don't be mean to the poor guy. He's madly in love with Mariana," Domani says, stealing a kiss on her cheek before kissing the baby's head.

"Fine. Well, why didn't you bring her with you?"

"She was sleeping."

"Please tell me you either woke her up to say you'd be out, or at least left a note or something for her," Aria asks while rolling her eyes.

"Yeah, I left a note on the front door," I explain, showing her I'm not a complete ass.

"Wow, you are an idiot. On the front door? I can't. Luigi, I need you to drive me over to Nero's," she calls out, shaking her head at me, but I'm not sure what I did wrong.

"I'm coming with you," my zia says. She turns to me when she realizes I have no clue how I fucked it up this time. "You left the note on the front door like you expect her to run away." Damn it. She has a point. If I'd left it in on her bedroom door that would have been smarter.

"Do you want me to take Luca with me?" Aria asks Dom.

"No, my queen." He loves having his boy with us. Twenty minutes later the women leave the house, and Dom and I head into this office to work on a game plan.

My heart thumps in my chest as we wait for the response from Paul Gordon. He's agreed to meet us at Domani's home, believing his men will protect him, but his men are pussies and will fall if they challenge us.

Inviting him here on the pretense of business was a mastery of skill, but the talk of massive profits drives motivation for most. He's a typical scumbag that needs to meet his maker, but I have to bide my time. We need more than his life at our feet. I want to find the players and crush them. When I think about my Mariana being a potential victim of his, my blood goes cold.

He preys on innocent women, making my stomach turn with the violent urge to rip his heart straight out of his chest.

"Calm down. We need him to come here on the pretense of business. If he sees you looking like a damn raving lunatic, it won't work out well."

"Sorry. The thought of him being even remotely close to Mariana pisses me off. I'm glad she's at the house instead of here."

"Don't worry. If everything goes according to plan, he'll never be a danger to her again," Dom says. Damn right. One way or another I'm getting my hands on Gordon and he'll be dead. Nico got that information to me right on damn time. I owe him and Bingo a lot because I wouldn't have gotten to Mariana in time.

"Do you think he's arrogant enough to come down here?" I ask, knowing I'll go looking for him either way, but the prick is bold as hell.

"Yes. Men like Gordon think they're untouchable. Plus, he's under the assumption that we're a small-time operation. It's good that I've kept an extremely low profile." We run so much, but it's all under wraps to keep the Feds and other officials off our backs.

"Well, we gave him the impression that the Bianchi family is crumbling under the weight of the new law enforcement in the area."

"Yes. He doesn't grasp the danger he's in."

"Nope."

A call comes to Domani's home number, which is a secure line. "Bianchi."

"This is Paul Gordon. My friend asked that we meet. I don't have much time today, but I will be near the Northside in an hour."

"That will do for us. I'm at home dealing with some personal matters, so I'll be here."

"Yeah, I heard you were married, but I have girls if you're looking for something sweet on the side."

"Maybe. Married life isn't all it's cracked up to be." A look of pure rage crosses his face as he tells that whopper. My cousin adores his wife. Fuck, Domani might kill him for even suggesting that.

"I've got the perfect lineup," Gordon says with a chuckle.

"We can talk when you get here. I worry about anyone listening in."

"Understood. Say no more."

Domani ends the call. "That was disgusting."

"Yeah, he's a natural-born pig. The thought of someone other than my Aria is revolting. Still, I have to play the game until I have him in my clutches."

"Then I get to play."

"That you do. Now, let us discuss other matters. I've got the distillery numbers to speak to you about." While we wait for the sick fuck, we handle our business; however, destroying Gordon plays in my head the entire time.

8

Mariana

THE MAN IS AN IDIOT. I wake up to hear him talking to a man. I keep out of sight and listen as best as I can. The man cheers him on for abducting me. I shake my head, but I suppose it's natural in the criminal world. When he leaves, he looks up at the stairs several times, appearing to be confused. Finally he writes a note and attaches it to the front door.

As soon as he's gone, I snatch it off the door.

I have to go to Domani's and didn't want to wake you. Please don't leave. — Nero

I don't know whether to laugh or swoon. The man is trying. Instead of thinking of leaving, I head into the kitchen. If he has a sweet tooth, I think I'll bake a cake or some dessert. I head into the massive pantry and look for some ingredients. This guy does have a sweet tooth. I dig through the pantry, and there are so many packaged treats: everything Hostess makes along with Reese's, and all kinds of chocolate. He needs something homemade for dessert. I pull out the ingredients to make him a pie.

The doorbell rings, and I head out of the kitchen to see who is here. Maybe I shouldn't answer.

Then the door opens to Aria and another woman who's a bit older. "Ah, there you are. I wouldn't have come in, but we weren't sure you'd know to open the door. The house is secure, so you don't have to worry about strangers. So this is my mother-in-law, Signora Bianchi."

"Hello," I say, blushing.

"She's gorgeous."

"Right? No wonder Nero's acting like an idiot."

"Please don't be mad at him for not telling you he was leaving."

"I got his note. Although, we're not that close, so it's not like he has to tell me where he's going."

"I told you she doesn't get how lost Nero is."

"She's adorable."

"Um… thanks. I was in the kitchen about to make a dessert for after dinner. Do you know what he'd prefer?"

"Well, it depends on what you have. He prefers fresh apple pie. I know my baby boy." Nero did say she was more like a mother to him than his own. I smile as she leads us into the kitchen. "So you're making him a dessert. I can't wait for the wedding."

"I'm sorry, Signora Bianchi, because he's not going to give you time for a big wedding."

"I don't have any family or friends to invite anyway."

"Ay dio, I just need a week. You kids. I'm calling your mother and we're going to get to work."

"Oh goodness. You're going to have a huge wedding."

"You know, Nero hasn't asked me and we hardly know each other."

"It's so cute how she doesn't think it's going to happen. You can stay with us if you want to avoid temptation. Nero won't bed you until you're his wife."

"What?"

"That's the vow the men in the family took. No putanas and no bedding your bride-to-be before the wedding." Aria goes on to tell me how their wedding was a last-minute change, but I'm still trying to put it together that they're telling me Nero's a virgin.

"Wait... are you telling me that Nero has saved himself for marriage?" I shake my head, not believing it.

"Yes. He has more reasons for it. His mother was a putana and she used his father and tried to make him betray his family. He only wants his wife to be in his bed."

"Oh." That explains the fact that he put me back into the guest room.

"I see the wheels turning in her head."

"I need to make the pie, and I don't know about the wedding. I'm not counting my chickens before they're hatched."

"Just so you know, I can be a bridesmaid."

"If that's the case, you can."

"Yay," she squeals, jumping up and hugging me.

We make the pie together for the next couple of hours, and it's a total blast. These women are amazing, and I'm grateful that they want me to be included.

We're just pulling the last pie out of the oven when Dom calls, saying he needs her to come home and to take care of Luca.

With a shrug of her shoulders, she says, "Okay. Come on, ladies, let's take pie to the men instead. We'll leave the second one for you two, but this will make their day. I'm sure whatever it is, the men are going to do something important."

"Are you sure I should go?"

"Why not? If he has a problem with it, tell him to fuck off."

"We're gonna be good friends."

"That we are." We leave the house, and Aria locks the door and then hands me the keys. I'm surprised, but I tuck them in my pocket and hop in the back seat. "Luigi, this is Mariana, Nero's future bride."

"Not yet," I say, reminding them it's not official in any way, shape, or form.

"Yes, I know who she is." He smiles at me, and I wonder if I'm the last person to learn of our impending marriage. As soon as we pull through a large steel gate, I spot a vehicle I recognize instantly. I hope it's not the case. "Um... who's car is that?" The license plates with "P. King" on them give it away, and I have my answer.

"The men have a guest. It's nothing that should concern you."

"Actually, it does. I can't go in there. Please, can you drop them off and take me back to the house," I confess, voice shaking as I duck my head down.

"Of course. Of course," Aria says, rubbing my arm to comfort me. "What's going on?"

"Nothing. It's just that he's a sleazebag," I tell her. It's all I really can say because of his threat to me, which was enough to send me running for my life.

"And Nero knows it, Miss Conlon," Luigi adds.

"Does he, though?" I challenge.

"Stay in the car and down. Ladies, I'll escort you in and take Miss Conlon back."

"Thank you," I whisper. They exit the vehicle, and then Luigi returns a minute later.

"Okay. Let's get you back to the house."

"Thank you. Please don't tell Nero I left the house."

"If you wish it."

"Are you just saying that?"

"No. It's not my business, and as my wife would say—a happy wife, a happy life."

"A smart man in the bunch."

"Thank you, ma'am." He drops me off and thankfully, Aria gave me the keys so I go back into the house and walk into the living room, taking a seat on the sofa. I need a break from all the drama that has encompassed my life the past few days. Since I met Nero, my world has been non-stop confusion mixed with nothing but riotous emotions. Despite knowing that my boss was in their home, I trust that it wasn't for a pleasant visit, and only added to the truth to Aria's words. Nero is willing to slay my dragons because he wants me to be his. Other than his actual profession, the man screams too good to be true.

I wait for him to come back, but as the time grows later, the doorbell rings. I look out, and it's Luigi. I open the door. "What's going on?"

"I've been summoned to inform you that Nero will be later than expected. He'll be giving you a new phone tomorrow, but for now he doesn't want you to worry. I've also brought you a dish from Giuseppe."

"Thank you."

"Do you want to come in?" I offer, attempting to come off okay, but I'm really not. I wanted to see Nero.

"No. I have to go home before my wife reams me a new one." He smiles and turns to leave.

"Did he say roughly what time he'd be back?" I call out, hoping that he has some sort of answer to give me.

Shaking his head, he frowns slightly before adding, "No, but it will be sometime in the wee hours of the morning."

"Okay."

"I'm sorry, but like I said, it's nothing to worry about."

"Thank you. Have a good night." He leaves the house, and I set the plated container on the table by the door. Looking out the window, I watch as Luigi pulls out of the gated drive and heads in the opposite direction of Aria's home. Well, what am I going to do with myself? I guess it's time to see what they brought me.

Taking it into the kitchen, I open the still-warm dish. It's a lasagna with a side salad and garlic bread. This family definitely knows how to eat. I pour myself a glass of wine and take a seat at the island to eat.

Once I finish, I clean the plate so I can return it tomorrow. Then, I decide to explore the house. It's a large home, but not as large as Dom and Aria's. Still, there are lots of doors. I didn't bother earlier because I thought Nero would be home sooner.

I find myself in the library, checking out the large stack of books that fill each and every wall from floor to ceiling. I never pictured Nero as a reader, but I guess I was mistaken. Maybe he's a collector. I stroll across until I get to a large sliding wooden ladder. Immediately, I climb on it and pull a Belle move, sliding along the bookcase. I nearly fall when it stops. No one tells you it's much harder than it looks. Climbing off before I break my neck, I begin to look for a book.

"Well, this isn't an easy task either." Finally, I settle on a crime novel and lie in the amazing settee to read.

9

Nero

"WE'RE SO glad to have you here," Domani says, stepping to the side and taking his seat behind his desk. "Please. Have a seat. Would you like a drink?"

"No, thank you. I got a call that your people wanted to meet with me to work on a deal." Good. I'm sure Dom's gritting his teeth, trying to remain civil. I'm itching to rip his head off.

"Yes. We have a beef with the Martinelli family, and well, we want to move in on their territory. They're appearing weak because they don't know you have dealings in their area."

"Well, they are slipping, but when empires get too big, they lose track of their money and they start to crumble." I growl, moving from my perch against the wall behind him.

"Yeah. We had a little problem like that recently."

"You didn't need to bring your goon in here."

"Nero's not my goon, as you put it. He's my second-in-command, so you will do well to mind your manners."

"Sorry. I just get jumpy when I'm outnumbered."

"I can sympathize with that." I toss my cousin a glare that the fuckhead doesn't notice.

"So, let's get down to business. We're looking to expand and clean house."

"What does this have to do with me?"

"Nothing, but we wanted to let you know because we wanted to make a deal." All I want is to end his life, but I plan to take some time, making him squirm before I end him.

"What deal?"

"We'll get the feds off your scent, but we want fifty percent of your business."

"Are you fucking nuts? The feds aren't onto me at all."

"That's right, you think because you have a couple police officers on the take that you're safe. We know otherwise. See, when our guy fucked up and started skimming from his deliveries, we checked into his personal dealings. Your name came up."

"I don't have anything to do with Eddie Walsh."

"We didn't mention his fucking name, so how the fuck did you know who we were talking about?"

"Um... see, that's because he's the only one who constantly owes me money."

"That's interesting, because we know that's not true. He pays you well because you've got him skimming from us, but that's not it. It's not why I've asked you here. You created a mess we had to clean up. We offed a beautiful woman named Mariana because she saw something she shouldn't have."

"She's dead? Fuck. I've been on the hunt for that bitch. She stole my money and didn't pay it back like she promised."

"Wait, are you the one who pretended to be her boyfriend to my contact?"

"Oh, you mean your cop friend who tried to get her back for you? You should know your officer buddy is under internal investigation. Did you know that?"

"Bullshit."

"Don't believe us, but he's in the middle of ratting you out to the cops to save his ass."

"He wouldn't."

"No? We have our own connections, and he's crossed too many lines that his people took notice of." I slip on my gloves quietly. I might be a big guy, but I'm stealthy.

"I can't believe it."

"Well, that's tough because it's true." I toss a rope around his throat and then Dom ties his hands with a zip tie. I loosen my grip just one inch to let him breathe.

The next words out of his mouth force my hand. Torture it is. "It's all because of that stupid bitch. She couldn't do a single thing right. I wish you would have let me hit that before you took her out. She was a fucking virgin." I lose control and strike him in the face.

Grabbing his face forcefully, I say, "I didn't kill her. She's mine, and the fact that you threatened her, insulted her, and then tried to find her means you crossed a line with me that's not acceptable."

"Come on. Take it easy. She's just a piece of ass, and you cost me a good two hundred thou on her virginity." I lose it and bash him in the face with my elbow.

"Enough, Nero. Do what is needed. Goodbye, Mr. Gordon. May God have mercy on you because Nero here will not." I lead the fucker out of the house with a gun to his head.

"Come on! We can work this out."

"No, we can't."

"I can give you information on anyone. I have it all."

"Start talking." He does. And for an hour all the way back to his club, which has had a sudden power outage and has been evacuated for safety, he spills his guts about more than his activities. I have enough information to sink several public officials who are aiding this piece-of-shit bottom feeder.

"We're here in your club. It's time to get out."

"What about my car?" This fool thinks I'm going to let him go. Nothing but death is good enough for this bastard.

"Relax, your car is right here." Tony D. pulls up beside us. "I'd make sure all your shit's there because Tony's a bit of a klepto," I lie. I just want his fingerprints all over his vehicle before I kill him. He climbs in and I know he's looking for his gun, but that's gone.

"Looking for this? Come on, now. Did you think he'd leave you with a weapon to shoot us with?"

"Get inside the club. We're not done discussing everything you've given me."

He does so like a fool, but the place has been set up for just what I need. Sliding a mask over my face, I welcome the several junkies just in time to do their part. My work is done forty-five minutes later, and we do our best to remove any traces of our presence. Tony D. takes off the fat suit he donned for his role as Gordon.

"Damn, that felt disgusting."

"Now, it's getting late, and I have to check in with Dom."

"You mean so you can get home as fast as possible so that the newest edition to the Bianchi family is well cared for."

"Damn right."

Once I brief Dom on everything, I creep back to my

house. It's already two in the morning, but I need to check on my queen. Did she get pissed and trash the place? I go inside, and everything is as good as it always is. I see the apple pie she made just for me. Dom told me that she'd gone out of her way to bake for me. Fuck, I have to make it up to her. I picked up the ring yesterday and I've been itching to give it to her, but right now probably isn't the best time. I go upstairs and into my bedroom, changing out of my clothes and hopping in the shower to wash away the filth from today.

Slipping on some boxers and a tee, I go to check on Mariana. Opening her door, she isn't in her bed. It's still made. "What the fuck?"

I grab my phone and call Luigi. I don't give a fuck how late it is. "Where is she?"

"She?"

"Yes. Where is Mariana?"

"I don't know. She was there when I gave her your message."

"How was she? Did she fucking freak out or something?"

"No. Not that I remember. She seemed calm. Do you need to go on the hunt for her?" he grunts, clearly asleep.

"I need to find her right now."

"Shouting down the house works." She yawns, looking like she just woke up.

"Never mind, Luigi." I end the call and turn my attention to her. "Where the hell were you?"

"I fell asleep in the library." I pull her into my arms to calm my racing heart. "Did you just get out of the shower?"

"Yes. I thought you left."

"You thought I left, so you showered?"

"No. I showered and then came to say goodnight to you and you were gone."

"Sorry."

"I'm going to kiss you right now."

"Okay." I lose control and slam my mouth onto hers, walking her backward toward her bed. I lift her up and put her in the center of the bed. Parting her legs, I grind my cock on her mound. "I missed the fuck out of you, angel face."

"I missed you too."

"Marry me."

"Yes." I slide the ring on her finger. "Thank you, bella mia." I grind my hips forward as I kiss her lips. She wraps her legs around my waist, rocking her pussy against my shaft and the pleasure's instant and too much to handle.

Freezing, I pull her legs off my body. "But I can't."

"Can't what?"

"We need to stop, or I'm going to fuck you right here, right now."

"Okay. Let's stop." She nods, kissing my chin and jaw.

"Okay," I agree even though I continue to kiss her and the second we come up for air, I lift her blouse over her head, revealing her perfect tits to my eyes. My hands massage one sexy breast while my mouth sucks on her fucking pebbled nipples. I grip each one and lavish attention back and forth, unable to quell the panic that sets in my bones. She can't leave if she's carrying my baby. I kneel and grab her shorts, tugging them off, taking her panties with them.

"Nero."

"Mariana," I utter in reverence. Her hands go to the hem of my shirt and she helps me pull it off. "I can't stop. Please tell me you understand."

"I need you, Nero."

"This is forever, Mariana. I'm not going to ever let you go."

"I love you, Nero."

"Please say it again," I beg her as I play with her soaked pussy.

"I love you," she moans.

"I love you so damn much." I kick away my boxers and line my cock up with her wet slit and slowly push my way into her tight channel. Claiming her as mine feels too damn good to care about breaking my promise and taking her innocence with mine.

She's going to be my wife anyway. Her thighs flex as she presses her feet into the mattress, arching for more. We fuck wildly like the newbies we are until I can't hang on any longer. Pinching her clit, I take Mariana with me, falling hard over the edge and shooting my load deep inside her womb.

"I'm sorry. I shouldn't have done that so soon."

"Don't worry. Your aunt and Aria's mom are already planning our wedding."

"Are they?"

"Yes." I chuckle and ask, "Do they know I'm not waiting weeks to marry you?"

"Yes. They said they only need a week."

"Good. Very good. Now, Mariana, I need you to know something."

"What's that?"

"It's hard to discuss. See. I've never..."

"I know. They told me about the Bianchi men and their promise. I'm sorry I made you break it." She cradles my face with her soft hands, I kiss her palms and then kiss her lips.

"You didn't make me do anything I didn't want to do. In fact, all I want to do is repeat it all again."

"Maybe in the morning?" she suggests.

"I'm suddenly very sleepy," I say; my orgasm wiping me

out. I pull out of her tight warmth with my cock still quite hard and covered in a mixture of her blood with our releases.

"Are you leaving me?"

"Never." I scoop her up and carry her to where she belongs.

We enter our bedroom and I close the door, locking it before leading her to our bed. "What are we doing here?"

"We're gonna sleep," I promise.

"But this is your bedroom."

"It's where you should have been to begin with, but I was afraid of how much I wanted you even though I didn't think you felt the same way." We slide under the covers, and she rests her head on my chest.

"I'm yours, Nero."

"Let's sleep." I reach over to the nightstand and grab my phone. I quickly send Dom a text, even though he's probably asleep. *Rule's broken. Wedding in a week, no later. Love you all.*

Congrats. About time. I'll tell Mama to get on with it. Goodnight.

10

Mariana

WAKING up in Nero's arms is the best feeling in the world. He holds me as though I'm the only thing that matters, so when I snuggle in closer, he tightens his grip. I kiss his bare chest and whisper, "I love you."

"I love you, amore mia."

"You're awake?"

"Yes. Good morning." He kisses my forehead before climbing out of bed. "I have to be out of the house in twenty minutes. If you call and I don't answer, it's because my phone will be powered down. I promise to call and if it's an emergency, let Tony D. know and he'll summon me."

I snap my fingers and shake my head. "Damn technology, hindering criminal activity."

"Actually, angel face, I'm going to my normal, legal nine to five, but I have half a dozen meetings this morning. If you need, I can give you my assistant's number."

"Assistant? As is in female assistant?"

"No, angel face. Carson isn't a woman nor is he into men

at least that I'm aware of, so you have nothing to be upset over. Besides, I've given myself only to you."

"True." It's crazy how my heart skips a beat every time I think about it.

"Now, if you'll excuse me I must get ready for my boring regular office job."

"Wow, so not all vicious killer... pity." I roll my eyes and spin onto my side with a little too much attitude, but as the bed shifts, I know I'm in trouble. Nero pounces on me with a growl. "Keep that shit up, and I'll kill that pussy again."

"Fine, I suppose I could behave for just a bit. I can't promise all day, though."

"Well, that's okay, but you know the women will be here to make wedding plans, so you'll be too busy to be trouble."

"You never know what I can achieve." I wink, and he slams his mouth to mine.

We kiss wildly before he pulls away with his dick rock hard and jutting out, tenting his boxers. I want to crawl to him and service him on my knees. I lick my lips, and he frowns. "Later, I'm going to make you pay for all the bad things you do, including looking at my cock like you're starved."

"I'm famished, but I suppose it can wait." He hisses before slamming the bathroom door shut. I giggle as the shower turns on. My poor man. I love it.

An hour later, Nero's gone and the ladies enter. I meet Aria's mom and immediately fall in love with her. She's wonderful, and so we go about planning the wedding, both disgruntled mothers begrudgingly hating that they only have a week.

"If we had more time—"

"We don't, Mama. Stop giving Mariana a hard time. We

can do this easily. Look what we did for mine with less than half a morning to prepare."

"We had some stuff already at our disposal," Mrs. Bianchi says.

"It doesn't have to be special. It's not like I'm going to know most people there, and I frankly couldn't care less about this whole thing."

"My dear girl, I'm sorry that you had a lousy go this past couple of years, but we want you to have something to remember." Mrs. Bianchi sighs, patting my hand.

"How Nero and I met is one hell of a memory."

"Yes, but it's not one you can share," Aria admits.

"True. What really matters is the dress and flower arrangements. Everything else can be generic, plain. Okay?"

"We can deal with that, I suppose," Mrs. Bianchi says, shoulders slumping.

The rest of the afternoon is spent looking at gowns and having companies schedule visits with the ones I like the most. Purple is the color that I want splayed around all the white. After that, I frankly don't care.

By the time they all leave, I'm completely drained so I grab a pop and a bag of popcorn and turn on the television.

Scrolling the channels, I hit FOX32 which has the news on right now. The image on the screen draws my attention so I listen in:

Owner of a local strip club dies inside his club, which has been permanently shut down due to illicit activities. Mr. Gordon was just about to be arraigned on kidnapping, prostitution, and human trafficking when his staff found his body this morning. Included in the raid was a local officer who also moonlights at the club as a bouncer. No one knows who else will be added to the crimes, but we believe that Mr. Gordon got off easy.

Any news on the victims of the trafficking? No news yet, but

*the police tell us that they have been taken to safe locations
including local area hospitals.*

I stand in awe. My boss owned a strip club and did all
those things?

So that's what Nero was doing last night. I might be a bit
sadistic because I find his brutality sexy. Having somebody
to protect me is a completely new and welcomed feeling. My
heart flutters, knowing that he needs to care for me.

I love him more and more, and that scares the piss out of
me. The fear of abandonment is strong within my soul. I
hope there's no way they can tie it to him or anyone in the
Bianchi family.

"What's wrong?" I spin around to see Nero staring at me,
trying to guess what the matter is.

He closes the distance in long strides, looking sexy as
hell in his dress shirt with the sleeves rolled up. With a kiss
to my lips, he pulls me down onto his lap as he sits on the
sofa. "Tell me, angel face, what's going on?"

"They just found my old boss dead, and he was a bigger
sleazebag than I knew."

"Yeah. I told you I'd take care of it." He cups my chin,
running his fingers along my jaw before replacing them
with his mouth. Embracing the tenderness, I almost forget
about our conversation. The sneaky bastard.

Nudging him slightly with a tone of anger in my voice, I
ask, "Is that why he was at Domani's yesterday?"

"You knew of that?" He pales and then straightens his
spine.

I wrap my arms around his neck and play with the edge
of his hair. This man is so gorgeous I steal another kiss
before explaining what happened. "Yes. When Domani
called Aria, we were all going to go over there. It wasn't until
we pulled up the driveway that I noticed the car. I had to get

out of there, so I asked Luigi to bring me back. Please don't be mad at him for not saying anything. I begged him to keep quiet."

"I'm not mad at all. He's a married man. He knows when to keep his mouth shut and when not to. The only person I'm upset with is myself. I'm sorry that I didn't think about that factor. I swear, I didn't mean to make you uncomfortable in any way."

"Thank you, but knowing he's out of my life forever makes me feel incredible. Does that make me bad?"

"Not at all. You were in danger with him alive."

"Thank you for slaying my dragons."

"No one will ever come between us."

"How about we have nothing between us?" I ask, kissing his throat.

"Sounds like a great idea." With a growl, he scoops me up and stands.

"Wow."

"Where are we going?"

"To our bed, where I plan to worship you until we're too tired to move."

11

Nero

IT'S OUR BIG, special day and I'm thrilled to fucking hell that it's here, although I have to say I'm pissed about last night. They took my wife away from me because I'm not supposed to see the bride before the wedding. I snarled and barked, but I lost in the end. Killing people with my bare hands is my specialty, but dealing with a bunch of angry women is a dangerous place to be.

"It's almost time, Nero. Calm yourself." Dom hands me a drink which I finish in one gulp.

"Easy for you to say. You're already married."

"And you have already bedded yours, so it's not like you're anxious to have your first time," he reminds me. It's not meant to be a dig, but that doesn't help my already anxious mood.

"No. I fucking miss her. It's the first time that I've spent the entire night completely away from her. I don't like it." It's stupid for me to panic, but the thought of her deciding I'm not good enough plays in my head with every passing second.

A knock on Domani's office door alerts us that it's time. I take a deep breath and open it, knowing she's ready to come to me and easing some of that anxiety. My angel face is going to be legally and eternally mine. There are no words for the rush of emotions that come over me. We exit into the large garden area where Father Falcone waits for Domani and me.

After shaking his hand, I take my place and wait for the music to usher in my bride. Zio has granted himself the honor of walking Mariana down the aisle since she has no one else. The patio doors open, and I'm doing my best to stay still as she begins her approach.

Mariana's breathtakingly gorgeous. Her long white dress fits her figure almost like it's one with her body. It's simple but elegant, and there's something in the way she moves that adds to its beauty. They finally reach me, but I pay my uncle no mind because my eyes are focused on my beloved Mariana.

"Angel face, you look incredible," I breathe out, taking her hand in mine before we turn to face Father Falcone. She releases her breath and smiles.

The ceremony is over in a blur as I look at my wife, grinning like a fool. I slip my arm around her waist, pulling her to me as I share our first kiss with Mrs. Nero Bianchi. It takes a tap on my shoulder to finally stop, and then I notice that it's raining, pouring down on us. Everyone runs to take shelter, but I shrug and kiss my wife until we're panting for air.

"Let me get you out of the rain." I cradle my love and make a mad dash out of the downpour.

Mariana laughs as I carry her through the house and

upstairs to the room I usually stay in when I spend the night. As soon as the door closes, she giggles and says, "Talk about a kiss getting me all wet."

"I bet it's not the rain between your legs. I'll make sure of it." With a growl, I pounce on Mariana like a wild tiger ready to strike. I grab the back of the dress and tear it to shreds. Fuck, she wasn't wearing a bra, so she stands in front of me with the tiniest of white lace panties and a pair of kitten heels.

"Luckily, Aria suggested a second gown because there was a chance of a storm."

"Yes, the storm ruined it. I'll stick with that story," I grunt, lifting her off her feet and lay her on the bed. Standing, I undress and watch Mariana's eyes focus on my ripped abs down to my rock-hard cock. Climbing onto the bed, I yank her legs apart. "I want to see how soaked you really are."

Slowly, I kiss her lips and slither my way down her licking and biting my wife. I run my fingers over the wet lace, teasing her mound as she tenses and shivers. Her need only drives me more insane. Her pussy's soaked and my tongue laps up her juices. "So fucking wet."

Mariana moans and rocks her hips, rubbing her sweet slit in my face. "Only for you."

"That's right, my wife." Pumping two fingers into her heat, I curl and flex each one to find her perfect spot until she comes undone. Her cries are only muffled by the pillow she brings to her face.

As I position myself between her thighs, I taste her lips and slam into her warmth in one fluid motion. We rock and grind, kissing wildly as sweat beads down my spine. I hold out until I take my angel face with me, watching her close her eyes and ride the wave. The roar that rips through my throat as I fill her with every last drop of cum could shake the roof. I'm sure there isn't a soul in this house who didn't hear me.

I pull out and lay on my side, staring at my beloved. "I live for you, Mariana."

"I'm always yours, Nero." Damn right she is. And if anyone tries to take her from me, I'll destroy them. My temper builds just considering the possibility, so I hold her close for a little longer when she shouts. "We have guests waiting for us." She sprints out of the bed, her round ass and perky big breasts jiggling, so I watch the show right in front of me with my hands behind my head. I love this woman.

We're over an hour late to our own wedding reception, but I don't think a soul minded. And I don't give two fucks if they do. I'm happier than hell, forever with my Mariana at my side.

EPILOGUE

Nero

IT's three months into our marriage, and I can't get enough of Mariana. She eases the stress of the day. Even though eighty percent of the organization is clean, it's hard work keeping it that way. I spend half my days in my offices at work, and the rest cleaning up little hiccups with the investment firm we operate.

Most of Mariana's time is spent with the girls and the babies. The library is her baby, and she's started to donate books as charity work that Aria assists with. However, most of her time is spent on her artwork. Aria's even gotten Mariana to start drawing simple designs, and my woman is taking to it like a fish to water.

Most nights I get home late, and she heats up my dinner, sitting with me as I eat, and we talk about everything and anything. At least that's how it starts off, but by the end of the meal, I have her sprawled out, thanking her for the delicious food. With a little one on the way, it's gonna be hard to get my dessert before she's in bed, but I can't wait.

It's almost Christmas time, and I'm trying to find the best gift for my wife. I'm not sure what she wants because my angel face has everything and doesn't want anything.

I'm tying my tie, preparing for a long day of business keeping me away from my woman.

"The library," I mutter, thinking of something surrounding that for the holiday.

"What about the library?"

"Nothing, just thinking about your favorite hiding spot," I lie. I want to surprise her with something special, but I have no other ideas.

"Hey, I can't help that I fall asleep reading. The books are good, but the settee in there is so comfortable I just relax."

"I love that you rest whenever you feel like it."

"So what's up with the library?"

"I think it needs a renovation." I toss the idea out there to get some feelers, but the look on her face makes me fucking laugh. After she stops appearing shocked, she's practically snarling at me.

"What! No. Do not touch my library, or I'll bite you."

"Do you promise?"

"On your nuts." Well, fuck. Time to retreat.

"Never mind. I'll leave it alone. So what's going on for today?"

"I have a doctor's appointment."

I look at her in surprise. "What? Why didn't you tell me?"

"I did, but you said you had a big errand to do for Dom, so I didn't remind you again."

"Shit. You're right. Can't you reschedule?" I hate that I have to do that to her, but hell if I want to miss anything to do with my wife and baby. She's my fucking queen and seeing our life growing inside of her thrills the fuck out of me.

"Do you really want to go?" It's of course my favorite thing to do next to being inside of her. Seeing our little one is one hell of a joy for me. I finally understand what Dom feels for his baby boy, Luca.

"Yes. Of course I do. I want to see our little bambino."

"Okay. If I can get it tomorrow, will that work?"

"Sure. I'll make sure to let Dom and everyone know that my beautiful wife and I need to go to the doctor."

"I love you, crazy man."

"I'm your crazy man."

"Damn right. So I'm guessing your phone is staying here?"

"Yes." She's grown accustomed to days when I have to leave and fuck someone up. When I get home, she makes me ice packs for my knuckles and then she gives me one hell of a massage and a blow job any man would kill for. I'm starting to think she gets off on the dark side of me. Well, if that's the case, I'll keep up the good work.

"So before you go, can I have a kiss?"

"Always. I'm never leaving without a taste of your lips." I love having a taste of her any which way I can. My body craves her all the fucking time, even when we're going at it like fucking bunnies.

"I woke up really horny this morning." The confession shoots through me like straight electricity, stiffening my cock almost instantly. Her honeyed cunt must be drenched with need, waiting for me to eat it up. I tug on my tie and undo my cuffs.

"I'm sorry, baby. Do you need me to take care of you before I go?" Her eyes brighten up while she nods. "How do you want it? Do you want me to eat your pussy? Fuck you deep and hard, or slow and gentle?"

"Do you have time?"

"I always have time to please my wife." She grabs the edge of her nightgown and lifts it over her head.

"Any way you give it to me, I'll be happy."

"That's what I want to hear. On all fours, angel face. I want you to feel it deep and slow, but first I want you to ride my face." I take off my shirt and pants, climbing onto our bed. "Bring your pussy to me." She straddles my face and I go right at her mound, licking her wetness, knowing with how heated she is that she's gonna come twice for me before I'm done with her.

She pumps her ass in my face, giving me a mouthful of her kitty. I eat the fuck out of her slit, licking and sucking on her nub until she's crying out my name. I'll never get enough of hearing her lose control and shout my name.

I tap her ass and lift her off me before jumping off the bed. She's in position with her sexy ass in the air because she's about to get mounted like a motherfucker. My cock throbs painfully in my boxers, and I need to bring us both to an explosive orgasm.

"That's it, angel face, play with those sensitive nipples while I get ready to make you cream again."

"Yes, Nero." I test her pussy, which is still fucking drenched. She lives in an insane state of perpetual arousal. Even my dick gets tired, but her pussy needs a pounding at least three times a day.

I kneel on the bed and tease her cunt from behind, dipping my finger in enough of her honey to play with her tight asshole. Running my tip down her lips, I coat it before sliding into her depths while my finger works her little ring. Leaning forward, I pump my dick in and out. "Fuck, Nero."

"Tell me—is it too much, or do you need more," I whisper along her spine.

"More," she says with a shuddering moan.

"That's right. You need to be under my control, don't you? Do I need to bring out the cuffs, my dirty little prisoner?" Since we've been married, I learned my wife has a very kinky side. She almost ached for me to take her that first day as punishment for seeing what she shouldn't have.

"No. I promise to be good," she pants, but I can feel the smile spread along her face.

"Liar," I growl in her ear, gripping her throat as I fuck her in a staccato rhythm, driving in hard and pulling out slow, repeating it until her walls flex, clenching around my thickness. I never hurt her, but she loves it rough.

"I promise."

"Tell me you're gonna do what I tell you."

"Always."

"Fuck, you're gonna make me nut in you. You want that. You want my cum deep in your womb, claiming it for my own, don't you?"

"Yes, sir. Come inside of me."

"I should come in your pretty ass for your little lies, but I don't have time to prepare you. Maybe I should lock you in this room so you'll behave."

"I'll behave. Please. Oh, fuck, Nero. I love you," she cries out, coming on my length.

I let out a roar and then grunt as I shoot my load. Tipping her chin, I tilt her head and kiss her lips. "I love you, my wife, my heart and soul, and my captive for the rest of our days." Keeping our bodies pressed firmly against each other, I hug her from behind as I rest on my heels.

"I can't wait for you to come home, and you haven't even left."

"I'll send Aria and Gloria over."

"Yay. Okay. You can go now."

"Keep it up, and I might tie your ass up to make sure you are really needy for me when I get home." I kiss her and slide out of her depths, turning her to lie on her back and relax as I hurry and wash my ass before she stops me again. God, I'm loving life.

EPILOGUE

Mariana

Ten years later…

NOT MUCH HAS CHANGED since I've become Mrs. Nero Bianchi, except that we have a whole army of boys: seven little men who are eager to run and roughhouse all day. This is the last pregnancy for me. I've already told Nero that. I don't even care if I have a girl or not, because we're not trying again. Nope. I will fuck that man all day and night, but one of us is getting fixed. My business can't handle another one of these little ones popping out.

I'm in the middle of cleaning up the house before we head out for the day.

"Mama, are we playing in Zia Aria's pool today?" my oldest asks. Our pool is being fixed after the motor broke, leaving the pool a disgusting mess in a matter of a day. Of course, we have limited warm days in Chicago, so it sucks when things like this happen. Luckily, Aria and Dom live down the road, so we can take advantage of these blisteringly hot days.

"Yes. I've packed your things. We're going to have a barbeque there."

"Ooh. Does that mean you're going to be making that sweet salad?"

"It's already made, Junior. You know your father." All of my boys take after him and have a sweet tooth that almost seems endless, although they understand that they have to eat all their vegetables first. Thankfully, they love them too.

I look at my oldest and see his daddy in him so much. Signora Bianchi showed me pictures of a young Nero, and Junior looks just like him, lanky and dark from playing in the sun.

"There you are. I've loaded the vehicle. Are we ready?" Nero says, taking my hand and pulling me into his arms for a sweeping kiss.

Once he finally releases me, I answer, "Where are the rest of the boys?"

"In the car. Tony's already taken half our little army over there. I'm just waiting for you two." I continue to pack the last of the stuff we need. I go to carry it and Nero scowls, snatching it off the counter before I can lift up.

"How come I was the last to know about the trip?" Junior huffs, crossing his arms. Being the oldest, he wants to be the lead and in the know on everything.

"Because you were busy sleeping in the library, just like your mama. Now come on, I have your swim trunks packed." Nero bends his finger, wagging it as he summons me to his side. His hand slips under my long swimming cover-up, opening it just partially. His eyes rake up and down my body, sending shivers through me. "Now—you are so damn beautiful, and you're lucky that it's gonna be just our family because that swimsuit could end a lot of men's lives today."

"You're nuts. I've gained weight again, and my belly is starting to show. It looks like I've had too much pasta."

"You'll always be sexy to me, and I will always be a possessive man, hoping you never escape."

"Just wait. I'll get out of this house when you're not around." I do it almost on a daily basis, but I'd never want to leave my love. Nero's everything to me. I live for him and our boys.

He chuckles and shakes his head, holding the front door open for me.

"Come on. The last one to the car has to help Daddy unload it." Junior doesn't rush to our vehicle. Instead, he holds the door open for me to climb in first. I nod and give him a kiss on his cheek.

Nero leans in and whispers to our son, "Such a good man." He smiles up at his papa and waits until I'm inside before getting into his side. I've raised gentlemen— dangerous gentlemen.

ABOUT THE AUTHOR

C.M. Steele is a bestselling author on Amazon with so many books to read and enjoy!
FOLLOW HER:
Website/Newsletter: www.cmsteele.com
Amazon Author Page: www.amazon.com/C-M-Steele/e/B00MQ9FPZS/
Facebook: www.facebook.com/CMsteele2014
FB Reader Group: https://www.facebook.com/groups/1190691734281008/
TikTok: www.tiktok.com/@authorcmsteele
Instagram: https://www.instagram.com/c.m._steele/
Twitter: https://twitter.com/Author_CMSteele
Bookbub: https://www.bookbub.com/authors/c-m-steele

ALSO BY C.M. STEELE

C.M. Steele is a bestselling author on Amazon with over 120 books to read and enjoy!

C.M. Steele's Book List:

Bianchi Crime Family:

Married to the Mob

Captured by the Mob

Owned by the Mob

Best Friends Series:

Always You

His Dirty Secret

Sleep Tight

A Best Friends Duet:

Picture Perfect

Instant Obsession

The Captive Series:

Luciano's Willing Captive

The Russian's Captive

Sergei's Stubborn Captive

The Caught Series:

Caught In A Case

Caught Off Guard

Caught in A Lie

Caught Crossing the Line

Caught Breaking the Law

Caught Red Handed

Cavanaugh Security Series:

Protecting Macy

Securing Blake

The Cline Brothers of Colorado:

Whatever it Takes

Taking Whatever he Wants

Finding Paradise

Dark Hearts Series:

Intense

The Falling Series:

Falling for the Boss

Falling for the Enemy

Falling Hard

Family & Friends:

Wanting it All

Chasing his Sunshine

Lassoing His Cowgirl

Ben's Resolve

Gimme Series:

Sugar

Luck

Rain

Cream

Heat

The James Family:

No Choice

No Way Out

No More Waiting

The Kane Family:

His Christmas Rose

Her Christmas Surprise

His Candy Kane

Christmas in July

Keepsakes:

Keeping Blossom

Keep in Mind

The Lamian Wars:

Bound

Reveal

Release

All Hallows Eve

Love Bites Series:

Love Bites

Once Bitten

The Middleton Hotels:

Built for Me

Built to Last

Built Strong

Built Over Time

Built Overnight

Nothing but Trouble Series:

Taking the Bait

Taking the Mafia Princess

Guarding Forever

A Steele Christmas:

Mason's Winter

Perfectly Wrapped

The Company You Keep

A Steele Fairy Tale:

My Gold

My Forever

My Property

My Prince Charming

A Steele Riders Family Novella Series:

Holiday Knockout

His Siren

A Steele Riders MC Series:

Boomer

Mick

Jackson

Doc

Beast

Ghost

Wrench

Blade

Southern Hospitality:

Down South

Gone South

Sweetheart's Treats:

Sweet Surprise

Doctor's Orders, Sweetheart

Sweet Surrender

Twin Sin:

Stalk Me Please

Sinful Intent

White Wolf Ridge Series:

Turner

Wolfe Creek Series:

Wolfe's Den

Beta: Her Alpha

Raging Kane

Written in History

Others:

Buying Love

Christmas in Camden

Conquering Alexandria

Grant's Deal

Hunting Allegra

Killer Abs

Love Discovered

Loving My Neighbor

Mrs. Valentine

My Christmas Gift

Rainy Days Stormy Nights

Red Hot Nights

Room Service

Scarred

Sharp Curves

So Wrong

Standing There

Stealing Beauty

Taking the Thief

The Wedding Guest

Unexpected

Manufactured by Amazon.ca
Bolton, ON